JUST CAN'T FALL
for the Enemy

a **Four Seasons Park** sweet romantic comedy

SASHA HART

Just Can't Fall for the Enemy by Sasha Hart

Published by Diamond Patch Press

P.O. Box 970982 Orem, UT 84057

http://sashahart.com

Copyright © 2022 Diamond Patch Press

All rights reserved. No portion of this book may be reproduced in any form without permission from the publisher, except as permitted by U.S. copyright law.

This is a work of fiction. Names, characters, places, and incidents either are the product of the author's imagination or are used fictitiously. Any resemblance to actual persons, living or dead, events, or locales is purely coincidental.

*For my girl, Savanna,
and our chick flick nights*

ONE

Sophie

I STARED at the man sitting in front of me—all 150 pounds of high breeding and expensive tailored shirt of him. He didn't stare back as he was currently too busy judging every inch of the restaurant with a frown. "So," he began, "why did you want to meet here again?"

It's the nicest restaurant in town. I didn't say it and prided myself on not throwing the entire basket of garlic bread at his face, tugging at the sleeve of my nicest blouse instead. "It's a good central meeting place. You're staying at the hotel, right?"

"If you can call it that." He sniffed. "What an . . . *interesting* place to live."

I felt my body tense and told myself to calm down. Huckleberry Creek, Montana, was the most charming small town in existence. The fact that he couldn't see it only proved this entire night—and the earlier twenty minutes spent straightening my hair—would be a waste of time. "You don't like small towns?"

He wrinkled his nose at a family with several children sitting nearby, all in worn yet clean clothes. "Let's just say these aren't my people. Obviously my mother has never set foot here, or she would have flown you to Chicago to meet me instead." His fork hovered over his plate of pasta, drawing my eye to a pair of cuff links. *Cuff links.*

I wouldn't have gone to Chicago for a date with a rich prince, let alone the whiny son of a senator. I'd only agreed to this blind date to make Grammy happy. Apparently, she and the senator lady were friends. Staring at this man and his permanent pout, I couldn't imagine why. His collar fell slightly open, just casual enough for the occasion yet perfectly fitted like a politician's speech outfit. Made sense, considering who his mother was. Everything about his appearance screamed, "Eligible and desirable man in search of a doting wife." Why he assumed me a candidate was beyond me.

"So, anyway," he said again. "Let's get on with it. What do you think a wife's role is in our society?"

I didn't ask what we were getting on *with*. He'd stared at his lap as he asked the question, just as with the last two oddly formal questions. He'd ordered for me against my insistence otherwise, claiming the online reviews praised this spaghetti. He forgot I'd grown up in this town. I knew every inch of it, including who probably made this and every detail about the server who brought it to our table. I'd even attended the opening of Alice's Italy House, for goodness' sake. The only reason a man would insist on ordering spaghetti for a woman was to test her breeding.

Well, two could play that game.

I shoveled a huge bite into my mouth, making sure one of the noodles hung over my bottom lip, and talked around the food. "Wives should live the same way as their husbands, doing whatever they want." I slurped the noodle into my mouth as messily as possible.

He frowned. "Even a senator's wife?"

"Especially a senator's wife. Sounds like a very lonely place to be if you ask me." I picked up the glass of ice water, brought it to my mouth, and slurped loudly.

He flinched and fixed his gaze on his lap again. "Uh, okay. Moving on. I wondered if you want children and, if so, how many?"

Yep. Definitely reading off a list. Now I was curious. Did he or his mother write it?

I took another bite, bigger this time. "Fourteen," I said with a full mouth. "Two to do the yard work, ten to do the cooking, and three for laundry. Then I can watch more episodes of *Abandoned on an Island*. Oh, and five dogs."

His eyes positively bugged now. "I . . . fourteen?"

"And five dogs," I repeated. "One pit bull, one Great Dane, one boxer, a poodle mix, and a Chihuahua."

"But pit bulls are dangerous."

A giggle nearly erupted from my cramping stomach—I hated spaghetti—but I contained it barely in time. "Not true. I have one, and he's never tried to eat a child. He did take a chunk out of a date's leg once, but we got him to the hospital in plenty of time. Oh, and I forgot the cats. I want to run a cat rescue with at least twenty."

"Stray cats?"

"The strayest of all strays."

I'd gone too far. His eyes narrowed in suspicion. "I want two children, a boy and a girl. No pets."

"Good for you." I also thought two was the perfect number, but I'd fake a heart attack before I admitted that to Mr. Perfect Teeth.

His mouth tightened in displeasure, and he looked down at his lap once more. "What instruments do you play?"

Seriously?

I shoved another bite in and chewed it with my mouth

open, being sure to roll it around for good measure. His eyes widened as he stared at the pasta hanging half in, half out.

"I have a harmonica," I said, though it didn't sound like English. "Oh! And a recorder, from third grade."

"Mm-hmm." His shoulders lifted and fell again as if he heaved a great internal sigh. I wanted to pump my fists in victory.

"Have you ever been on TV?" he asked.

That one was easy. "Heavens, no. Nor do I ever want to be. I like my privacy, thank you very much."

His eyes flashed with something I couldn't read. "Shame. You have the figure for it."

He was honestly flirting with me right now? I could just walk out, but then he would have won. This date needed to end, and I needed him to be the first to surrender.

Time for drastic measures. Embarrassing ones.

I picked up my fork and scooped as much spaghetti as it would hold. When the fork was full, I lifted my knife and used it to support the pasta that remained, letting the giant spaghetti nest hover inches from my mouth.

The man's eyes went round.

I smirked and opened my mouth as far as it would go, shoving it all inside at once. The noodles dribbled down to my neck, splattering marinara all over my shirt and, to my satisfaction, one of his pristine cuff links. "Mmm," I moaned around the food. "So goot."

My stomach lurched, but it was worth it to see him lean back as if trying to put more distance between us, pure horror written across his face.

I eyed his plate. "Ah ooh going to eah that?"

He went green as I brought his plate closer and started to dig in. Then I grabbed my glass, which he'd filled to the brim—test number two and the first thing that tipped me off to his little test—and sipped it as loudly as I could, emitting a sickly slurping noise. A little girl giggled from the booth behind me. Most of the restaurant had gone quiet, I now realized, and watched with huge grins. They weren't this man's people, but they were most certainly mine—and they knew I had their backs tonight.

He closed his eyes and gritted his teeth. "H-have you ever been to a black-tie event?"

He was *still here*. How far would he make me take this? I thought quickly. "Only once, but not as a guest."

His shoulders tensed. "A waiter?"

"No, no. I was the entertainment." I picked up my glass, chugged half of it, and summoned my high school belching skills. It came at will—an eight out of ten but still acceptable.

The entire restaurant went still, the only movement coming from the man sitting behind my date, facing the other way in his booth. His shoulders began to bounce, his hand to his mouth to contain his laughter.

I wiped my mouth off and sighed loudly. "What do you think? Dessert?"

"I have to go." My date bolted, his face as green as the bush outside our window. The bell dinged as the glass door slammed shut behind him.

The restaurant's occupants began to roar with laughter. The little family's father came over to slap me on the back. "Best shutdown I've ever seen, Sophie. They'll be talking about this for years."

"To Sophie," a woman said, raising her glass of Diet Coke.

Most of the room lifted their glasses to the ceiling, including the little girl with her juice box. "To Sophie."

I stood and gave a little curtsy. "Enjoy your night, everyone. I don't think we'll be seeing him again."

As the father returned to his seat and the room resumed conversation, I let myself relax.

You could have just walked out, I chided myself. That would have been the more mature thing to do. But stalking out of a bad date didn't have the same . . . pizazz as driving him dramatically from town. And this had been far worse than a bad date. Drastic measures, indeed.

The man in the next booth stood, turned around, and gave a slow clap. "Well done."

Oh no.

I swallowed. This man was everything my date wasn't—casual, with short, dark-brown hair styled in a messy yet trendy way; comfortable jeans; and an open plaid shirt with a white undershirt that emphasized his strong build. A light, well-trimmed layer of stubble covered his chin. He wore sunglasses despite the setting sun outside. Something about him seemed oddly familiar.

"Thank you," I said, still standing awkwardly by the messy table. My stomach suddenly rumbled, begging to empty itself of the contents I'd just inhaled. I had thirty seconds to a minute, tops. I found a fifty-dollar bill in my purse and tossed it next to my plate, hoping it would be enough. I'd have to call Alice tomorrow and apologize for tonight's scene.

"Do you always drive obnoxious dates off in such an entertaining way?" the attractive stranger asked, dropping a wad of cash onto his own table.

Uh-uh. The handsome stranger was not following me out, not now. Even his voice seemed familiar somehow. Where had I met him before?

"Only in Italian restaurants," I said. "He should have chosen Chinese."

He frowned. "Are you all right? You don't look well."

My stomach turned over again. "Excuse me," I said,

sprinting for the restroom, which was, thankfully, unlocked. I heard his chuckle even through the door.

When I emerged ten minutes later, he stood where I'd left him. Lovely. He handed me my fifty back and closed my hand around it, his touch electrifying my entire arm. "You shouldn't have to pay for that jerk. Consider this my apology for the less-mannered of my gender. What's your name?"

I cleared my throat, relieved I'd been able to find some mint gum in my purse, but all that came to mind was a replay of tonight's events. The fourteen children and cats and dogs and the spaghetti . . . curse that limp pasta to the sky. I wouldn't be eating pasta again for a very long time. And the belch—*that* would be very hard to explain away. My traitorous face flamed again.

"Think of me as the dinner entertainment," I said, shoving the crumpled bill back at him. "You shouldn't have to pay for him either. Believe me, it was a pleasure to drive him from my town. Men like that don't belong here."

"Oh? Are you the town's designated protector?"

I thought about my young friend, Nate, and felt my determination surge. "Something like that."

He rejected the offering, shaking his head. "Please. It's the least I can do." He looked me up and down, making the heat in my cheeks creep down my neck. I'd scrubbed at the spaghetti sauce on my blouse, but patches of pink stubbornly remained. What kind of impression had I given him and everyone else in this room? And yet . . . he now wore a look of approval. Maybe even admiration. Was that a hint of red on his own neck?

An urge for my bed and a pint of Mintee's ice cream overcame me. "Thank you, then. Glad you enjoyed the show." I brushed past him to the parking lot and my car. I'd parked near the back, of course, impossibly far away.

The man actually followed me. "Question. If a guy met you at a Chinese restaurant, would he have a better chance?"

No, no, *no*. This was not happening. Not with spaghetti-sauce stains and probably puke on my blouse.

My car beeped as I hit the button on my key fob, and I yanked the door open to slide in. Then I gave him a tight smile. "I don't know that I'll be going on any more dates for a while, thank you." *Or eating dinner again, for that matter.*

"Wait." His voice held an edge of surprise. "You really won't tell me your name?"

After that scene? Not a chance. Besides, he was obviously passing through. With any luck, I'd never see him again. "Have a good night."

He unlocked his own car—an expensive red coupe, of course—and stood there watching me with little expression as I drove away.

TWO

TANNER

A LIGHT CHILL hung in the autumn air as I watched the woman go.

What was that about?

I stood next to my car longer than I should, half hoping she would come back, but her taillights disappeared in the distance. I recalled her little show inside and chuckled again. She'd put her date in his place without a single rude word. Impressive, especially since the guy acted like we were still living in the 1950s and women were expected to push out babies and have dinner on the table by five. I'd had half a mind to say something, but it hadn't been necessary.

Most of the gorgeous ones would rather die than put on a performance like that. What confidence. And I didn't even know her name.

A crowd gathered at the restaurant window, some with hands cupped to see better. Clearly, a few of the restaurant-goers had figured out who I was. My cue to leave. I folded my six-foot frame into my fusion-red Tesla. My car stood out in this town, no doubt. But that was part of the reason I bought it. A gift for myself after I received my first $100,000 paycheck. There had been many of those since, all piling up in my checking account, waiting for the day I knew what to do with them. It wasn't like a guy who'd spent the past four years traveling needed a mansion or a garage full of cars.

Maybe an apartment, though. Someplace to call home. And companionship that didn't require autographs and selfies at every turn. My dating life was, unfortunately, choppy and disconnected these days—the product of a career that kept me on the move. Probably better that the woman hadn't given me the time of day.

This is the life you chose, I reminded myself. *Most people would kill for the money you're making.*

As I drove down Main Street, I couldn't help but admire its charm. On the left was a park filled with benches, walkways, and loads of enormous trees that looked even older than the town. Strings of lights gave it a romantic air with the darkening sky above. On the far side of the park stood a gazebo beneath which sat a quartet of musicians in casual dress, as if they'd spontaneously put this together. The song that floated on the air sounded slightly twangy, like an old country ballad. An older couple danced on the grass below. With its tree-lined streets and the leaves turning brilliant shades of red, yellow, and orange, Huckleberry Creek was practically a movie set.

And I would be the first YouTuber to feature it.

A wave of nostalgia rushed through my veins. A long time ago, I'd had different plans—college, followed by a steady job. Then a friend's move and invitation for me to join him in Costa Rica became the perfect opportunity to ditch my local community college for a different kind of adventure. I started my travel channel—not the boring, informational kind but a show revealing the lesser-known tourist gold of various destinations. Before long, brands asked me to promote their stuff in exchange for hefty paychecks. Now, after only a few years of work, my channel had nearly twenty million followers.

It had become my career whether I liked it or not. Mostly I liked it. I'd even asked my assistant, Jill, to reach out to another popular YouTuber star, Guy Hadley, to see if he wanted to collaborate. So far, he hadn't given me a glance, and I didn't blame him. He was the most popular YouTuber on the planet with hundreds of millions of subscribers. He'd even appeared in a movie recently. Hooking him into a collaboration would launch my channel into the stratosphere. Success like that would be impossible for anyone to ignore, including my deadbeat Dad who was currently who-knew-where.

I flung the thought away in distaste. My career had nothing to do with him. Or my life, for that matter.

"Welcome to Huckleberry Creek," I began, speaking into my phone. "Small Town Central, USA. Population 1,100. Or maybe five hundred if you don't count the stray dogs. My first impression is that—"

A shadow appeared on the road.

I slammed on my brakes just in time. A doe stood there, ready to spring, watching me curiously.

I uttered a curse under my breath. "Where did you come from?" Her ears flicked back and forth as if she heard me, though she didn't move an inch. Apparently she didn't want me returning to my hotel anytime soon.

"You were this close to becoming deer jerky, lady dude," I told her, holding up my thumb and index finger to indicate an inch, though the animal didn't seem to care. She stared at me for a long moment before continuing on her way, heading for the shops across the street like she had a bag of cash and time to spare. I ended the recording and blew out a breath to steady my nerves. I would delete that last clip and start again tomorrow. Thoughts of the woman at the restaurant filled my mind, making it impossible to think about my channel right now. The way her brown eyes flashed when she spoke and the twinkle in them had me wishing I'd asked her out rather than just hinting at it. But then, I would only be here for six days.

The last thing I needed was another person to say goodbye to.

Someone behind me honked, and I flinched, checking my rearview mirror. The deer was long gone, and I looked like a doofus hanging out in the middle of the road. I stuck my hand out the window and waved. "Sorry," I called out and took my foot off the brake.

The second I arrived at the hotel and plopped onto the hard bed, my phone rang. "Tanner Carmichael," I said without bothering to glance at the screen. My focus was on the moth fluttering around on the ceiling. How did that get in? Probably the window. A terrible draft blew through from the ill-fitted frame, which looked like it had been installed in the 1800s.

"You're not going to believe this," Jill said.

My pulse quickened at hearing my assistant's voice. She must have heard back from Guy Hadley. "Try me."

"He's interested." There was a note of excitement to her voice but also an edge of hesitation.

I stamped down the thrill inside at her news. "But?"

"He likes your stuff, but he wants to see more than just places and history. He wants a video that feels more personal. Something with drama and authenticity."

I was confused, but Jill went on. "He wants something that features the people within the city—their stories and why they chose to live there and what it's really like."

"So he wants me to completely change my content." My first response was to get angry. Who did this guy think he was? I had twenty million followers. That wasn't a number to joke about, especially since gaining subscribers was becoming much more difficult these days. Of course, there were several influencers who had more than I did. A lot more. But most didn't even come close to my numbers.

Jill paused. "Maybe not permanently. I think one solid episode would do the trick."

My pride still smarted at Guy's critique. I wasn't sure I wanted to change anything, let alone the very heart of my channel.

"I'll call you back," I said and hung up.

I wasn't a diva and never had been. Brands had turned me down before, and that was fine. But this was different. I really wanted to collaborate with Guy. Or at least I needed him if I wanted to continue to grow my business. And I did—more than anything. I couldn't say why, but the more success I had, the more I craved. Bigger, better. Higher. That hunger kept me going on the hard and lonely days. Besides, my videos were art, each one feeding into the next, like I was telling the story of the location for my viewers.

Grumbling my frustration, I tucked my phone into my back pocket and hopped onto my computer to do a little research on Huckleberry Creek. Not much to find. It was the one problem with randomly choosing my locations on a map in front of millions of people—I had no idea what I would find there, if anything.

Clearly, I wouldn't be compiling a script based on what I found online. I needed to recruit a local to help, someone who knew the town well and loved it fiercely. Someone acquainted with every single one of those 1,100 people who made their lives in Huckleberry Creek. Some well-respected person who knew their stories.

Someone like the woman from the restaurant.

I thought for a long moment, took out my phone, and texted Jill.

I'm in.

THREE

Sophie

When my brunette model of a best friend and roommate walked in, she found me with knife held high, ready to stab downward.

"Don't do it!" Carmen cried, giggling. "I love you forever."

"Sorry. I have to." With a grunt, I plunged the plastic knife into my salad in an attempt to cut the hard meat—and promptly broke it with a snap.

We broke into a fit of laughter, and she dropped her purse onto the table. "Where's mine?"

"This *was* yours. Now it's mine." I shoved the entire wad of meat into my mouth.

Her lips curled into a pout. "Not my Mexican salad."

"Mm-hmm."

"The date was that bad?"

"Mm-hmm." I swallowed. "But don't worry. I bought you another one. It's in the fridge."

"You bought one and then ate my leftovers?"

"I only wanted a little bit, but I knew you were looking forward to finishing this off, so yeah. I got you."

Now she plopped herself into the chair across the table, knocking over her purse but not seeming to care. "You didn't even eat dinner?"

"Worse. I ate the whole plate in five minutes and then puked it up. I'm just now getting my appetite back."

Her nose wrinkled. "Seriously? Food poisoning or . . . ?"

"A ridiculous man who needed a lesson. Long story." I stared down at my salad and set my fork down, my stomach still feeling a little queasy. Maybe this wasn't such a great idea after all. "And then I had to run to the bathroom in the middle of a conversation with this other guy who saw the whole thing. He probably drove home laughing the entire way in his fancy red Tesla."

Carmen sat back in her chair, impatiently sweeping her long brown braid over one shoulder. She looked like a billboard ad even when she did that. "Red Tesla. A tourist?"

"Must be. I don't know anyone around here who would drive one of those." Our small Montana town attracted tourists but mostly Canadian ones seeking a quick getaway over the border and a weekend on one of our half-dozen crystal-clear lakes. Most of America hadn't discovered us yet, and I liked it that way.

Carmen thoughtfully drummed her fingers on the table. "Grammy Marissa texted me while you were gone. She asked if I knew how it was going. She didn't dare call you. I think she didn't want to disturb your romantic vibes or whatever."

"More like gastrointestinal discomfort and public humiliation. I can't set foot inside Alice's Italian House for at least another year. Worth it, though, to see the look on the guy's face. Do you know he had a list of questions hidden in his lap? *Do you want children?* Check. *Do you attend black-tie formal events often?* Big, fat X."

"No!"

"Dead serious. I felt like a horse being graded at auction."

"That's one I've never heard. Not surprised considering how nutty his senator mother is, though." Carmen's smile turned mischievous. "And the other guy—the tourist you talked to afterward?"

I had to rein this in, and quickly. "Tanned, well-dressed, throwing around money. Nice enough, but I wasn't in the mood for flirting."

She looked at me like I'd spouted off in Latin. "Why would that matter if he's hot?"

I snorted. "Because I had spaghetti all over my shirt and who knew what else? I had to make quite the scene to ditch the first guy. I didn't know it would attract a second."

"You're avoiding the question. Hot or not?"

I held back a snarky retort and bit my lip to hide a grin.

"That's what I thought. Otherwise you would've run to your car instead of talking to him like you do after putting in your time at every social gathering ever."

"I do not."

"Fine. The ones with men, then. Which are still most of them. But if you think you're getting out of Tess's wedding this week, you're dead wrong."

"I would never miss that, and you know it."

Her eyes twinkled like she didn't believe me. "I want all tonight's details after you finish your salad and, um, change your shirt. In the meantime, are you calling Grammy Marissa, or should I? Because I promised one of us would text her back, and it should definitely be you. Maybe you can convince her to lay off the blind dates for a while."

"Not for a while. Forever." This was the fourth date she'd forced upon me since leaving the family home to me and moving to Florida. Grammy meant well, but it was time for her to stop feeling guilty about abandoning me for sunny beaches and trying to make up for it by finding me companionship. She'd never understood my obsession with the beautiful Montana wilderness and its solitude.

Dating had only ever filled my life with misery, pain, and reminders of the love my parents shared before the accident took them away forever. The only joy I experienced these days came from my work in the national forest, its heavy silence broken only by the chatter of birds, and the occasional search-and-rescue missions that pulled me out of the entrance booth and into nature.

Okay, the dark-green uniform wasn't my favorite either. But it was still a hundred times better than a desk job.

"Oh," Carmen said softly, her eyes growing round.

"What?"

"I just remembered something. You said a red Tesla?"

"Dark red and without a single imperfection."

She made a clicking sound with her tongue. "I think I know who that was, but you aren't going to like it."

"Who?"

"Tanner Carmichael."

It sounded familiar, but again, I couldn't place it. "Okay, but who's that?"

She gave me an incredulous stare. "Really? You haven't seen *Tanner Carmichael Travels the World* on YouTube?"

I strained to remember. "I think I've seen an episode or two." My job kept me too busy for TV. A memory of the stranger at the restaurant rushed back to greet me—his practiced smile, his too-perfect outfit, the way he'd thrown around money like it was nothing. "So he's popular, I assume."

"Only one of the hottest stars on YouTube. And I do mean *hottest*. The entire town is buzzing about him since he went inside the gas station, asking if they had a way to charge his car.

I think he ended up using the charging unit in McPhearson's garage." She laughed.

"Wait," I said, remembering something I'd recently read online. "He's the star whose fans follow him around, right? Like, they race to a city he's just featured and consume it. I've heard horror stories."

Carmen shrugged. "I guess. I can totally see crowds of women chasing him around. I can't believe he flirted with you at the restaurant!"

He *had* flirted with me. Just like Alan had a few years ago, sweeping into my life and charming everyone in town . . . before delivering a blow that we still hadn't recovered from. If I stayed away from big events with men, from *strangers,* it was because I'd learned my lesson.

I would never subject my town to someone like that again.

Shaking my head, I shoved my—Carmen's—salad away. "No. Not a chance. He is *not* ruining our little town with his millions of followers and piles of cash."

Carmen hesitated. "I mean, I would take the cash part—"

"Who does he think he is?" I snapped, rising to my feet. "I know his type. He won't be happy until every mountain is paved over in expensive resorts, all paying him a hefty percentage for a single mention on his show because he has a pretty face and a charming voice. Our lakes will be too filled with entitled tourists to go boating ever again. They'll overrun the national forest and destroy the ecosystem. This is a disaster."

"A disaster? And you say I'm the dramatic one. You should have chosen a career on stage."

I barely heard her. The last thing Huckleberry Creek needed was another ladies' man who took what he wanted and left a trail of destruction and broken hearts in his wake . . . including mine.

Carmen saved the salad from launching off the edge of the table and carried it to the countertop for safety. "Well, they said he charmed most everyone at the gas station. He left Gwynn positively fanning herself. He probably went to get dinner right after that."

"Well, I hope he enjoyed the show." Where was my plastic knife when I needed it? "If I see him again, I'll send him and his Tesla packing. As in, I will pack him into the Tesla myself—the trunk if I have to."

"I'm sure. Just get his autograph for me first, will you? I may have seen a few or, you know, forty of his episodes."

When I whirled on my friend, she laughed. "Come on. You're going to look him up after this, and you know it."

Maybe I would, but only because I needed to know what I was dealing with—find his soft spots, his weaknesses. His very presence meant a threat to my sanctuary and everything that brought me happiness. Tanner could find another town for his travel show, far away from here. Huckleberry Creek was sacred. Mine.

All I had left.

I'd driven one obnoxious outsider out of my town tonight. It wouldn't take any effort at all to drive away a second.

FOUR

TANNER

I slept very little that night, too wired for any real rest. After taking a lukewarm shower and skipping the shave, I grabbed breakfast downstairs. Minutes later, I sat on the lopsided bed with my laptop open to Guy's latest episode about a child with leukemia in Detroit. Though I didn't want to admit it, he certainly knew how to pull on a person's heartstrings.

My phone buzzed, pulling me from my thoughts. It was a text from Jill. *Guy emailed again to say he's looking forward to seeing your next video. Don't let yourself get distracted this time. There's a lot riding on this one. Get it done, Tan!*

I disliked when she or anyone called me Tan. And I wasn't a fan of extra pressure. "Thanks for the pep talk, Jill," I muttered as I texted a quick thanks.

My first order of business was returning to the Italian restaurant. Someone there had to know the woman's name and where I could find her. But when I pulled up later that morning, all the lights were off, the cheap Closed sign in the window hanging by a thin chain.

"Something I can help you with?" a round woman in her

fifties asked, coming up behind me. She wore a gray dress with a white apron and a name tag that said "Alice," keys dangling from her hand. Suddenly, her eyes widened in recognition, and I realized I'd forgotten to grab my sunglasses on my way out. She clapped her hands. "You're Tanner Carmichael. My staff said you were here last night, but I had a christening to attend so I missed you. I hope you had a pleasant time."

"Every second of it," I said honestly. "So you didn't see last night's little show."

"No, but I heard about it. Pretty sure the entire town's laughing about it today. I hear the man's face was pretty comical. He won't be returning anytime soon." She unlocked the door and held it open. "What can I get for you? It's on the house, of course. Especially if you mention my place to those followers of yours."

I'd already put her restaurant on the list, but I wasn't looking for free food. "Actually, I'm trying to find that woman from last night. Can you tell me who she is and where she lives?"

Her eyes narrowed in suspicion. "What do you want from her?"

As protective as last night's acquaintance was of her town, it seemed they returned the favor. It only made me like the town more. "I only want to ask her a few questions. We tried to have a conversation afterward, but she wasn't feeling well."

She sighed. "Her name is Sophie, but I'll let her tell you her last name. Have to protect my kind, you understand. She's probably at work. Drive down the highway toward the national forest. They keep her crammed up in that entrance fee booth, heaven knows why. She'd be the best forest ranger in the world if they'd let her."

I had no idea what she meant by that, but the woman's name echoed in my mind. *Sophie.* "I appreciate it."

Alice looked past me to my parked car. "What about your team? Do they want to sample anything?"

"I don't have a team. I work alone."

She shook her head in disapproval. "Sounds like a lonely job."

"It's my brand. People like it."

"Maybe so, but it's your life, not theirs." She walked inside and threw a wave. "Good luck with Sophie."

"Thanks," I said, looking past her to the spot where Sophie had rejected me last night. And then she'd rejected me again in the parking lot, refusing to tell me her name. That wasn't something that happened every day. What made me think I could convince the woman to spend six days showing me around when she wouldn't even tell me who she was?

The door shut behind Alice. *Good luck*, she'd said, an amused tone behind the words.

Something told me I would need all the luck I could get.

FIVE

Sophie

I LEANED FORWARD on the metal stool and tugged my forest-green uniform shirt down over my hips. It never quite stayed where it was supposed to. My booth felt unusually hot for the end of September, and the open window didn't help much without a breeze. I grabbed the broom propped in the corner and started sweeping outside, a silly feat at the edge of a national forest but better than slowly baking my guts inside. I kept my ear tuned for the sound of Paul's battered truck approaching. The last thing I needed was for Paul to see me, the woman he refused to let outside the booth and into nature, doing something so . . . domestic.

Three vehicles approached from the direction of town, each with a sticker on the windshield. I returned to my booth and waved them on. The fourth stopped at my window. As I leaned out, my stomach flopped.

A red Tesla.

I resisted the urge to smooth my messy bun. I was a forest ranger, for goodness' sake, not prom queen.

Tanner Carmichael rolled down the window and leaned

out, resting his elbow in a way that flaunted his biceps. He wore the same grin as last night, as if he knew a secret and wouldn't reveal it. "Hello again, Sophie."

I barely contained a groan. I'd planned to chat with some of the more, shall we say, *vocal* members of the town today about how dangerous his presence was. If the warning spread far enough, hopefully he wouldn't be able to charm the town of Huckleberry Creek into cooperating. But now, as I saw him in the daylight, sitting in his fancy car, I knew convincing anyone of that would be difficult. There was something so disarming, so open and honest, about his smile. It was probably exactly that smile that wrenched my name from some unsuspecting person in town. *Traitor.*

"I came to beg a favor," he said.

I glanced back at the truck pulling up behind my booth. Paul. *Great timing.* "Unless this favor involves a week's pass to the park, it'll have to wait."

"As a matter of fact, I do need one of those. How much?"

"Forty-six dollars."

Tanner fumbled with his wallet and whipped out a wad of cash, which he held out, pinched between two fingers. I took it, ignoring the inner thrill as his fingers brushed mine. Three twenties. I'd have to get him change.

As I opened the register, he cocked his head. "I worried about you last night, driving off when you weren't feeling great."

"Well, I'm fine today. No spaghetti in sight." My stomach did another flop at the thought.

"Glad to hear it."

I handed him the change and his receipt, careful not to touch him this time. "There you go. Have a good day." *Please go away.*

"Tanner Carmichael," my boss said, hurrying over to shake

Tanner's hand. "I heard you were in town. Are you featuring Huckleberry Creek next?"

"That's the plan." Tanner fixed his gaze on me, sending another jolt of electricity down to my heels. *Stop it.* "Actually, I came to see if Sophie would consider showing me around town for a few days while I put this episode together. If it doesn't interfere with her work here, of course."

Paul glanced at me, his mouth pressed into the closest resemblance of a smile I'd ever seen. "It's been awhile since she took any vacation days. I suppose we could do without her for that long."

I gaped. Was the guy actually asking my boss rather than me? "I'm not a truck to be borrowed. I like my work here, and I have no desire to play tour guide to celebrities."

Paul snorted. "Don't be foolish. You're doing an important work for the park. The more visitors, the more federal funding we get and the more of a difference we can make here."

As if Paul cared about that. His priorities included sustaining the patriarchy of the National Forest Agency above all—men at the top, women at the bottom. Or *woman,* I should say, since I was the only one he'd ever hired. Back then, I'd considered this my dream job—spending the day in nature, working with animals, preserving the environment.

Ha. Funny.

Word was he'd be retiring in a few weeks, though, and passing his position along to Kenneth Vawdry. The new hire would have to take my place here, freeing me to *finally* perform the duties I actually wanted to do. Which included pretty much anything outside this booth.

But as restricted as I felt here, I kept my personal life under an even tighter rein. A celebrity bent on using us to further his career had no place in it whatsoever. Now that I knew what he intended to do here, I wanted no part of his little scheme.

"What exactly do you want to see?" I asked coolly.

"Just the spots only the locals know about. You know, insider stuff. Your favorite places, why you chose to live here." He grinned, sporting teeth just as straight and white as Senator's Son but somehow looking more natural. "The pasta is surprisingly good, but I'm guessing it isn't reason number one."

A sudden thought stopped me from rejecting him outright. If I told him no, he'd only turn to the first person in town who threw themselves at him. Lucille Morena, for one. She'd show him a *great* time—just like she did every other male tourist who came slinking through here in need of one-night companionship. The thought of her hanging on Tanner's arm made me see red, though I didn't want to explore why.

Both men watched me expectantly, waiting for my answer.

It was simple. If I said no, someone else would say yes. And she'd show Tanner all the best spots before his departure, leaving our town to take the fallout. But if I agreed . . .

"How much do you know about Huckleberry Creek?" I asked innocently.

He shook his head. "Hardly anything. I couldn't find much online, so it's all up to you."

My plan snapped together like a set of plastic building blocks. Instead of the highlights, I would show him the worst—all the rough and questionable parts. I would sabotage his entire week, and he wouldn't even know it. I would convince him Huckleberry Creek was the last place he should recommend to his tourist followers.

Do my job well and I would see his fancy taillights leaving town by this time tomorrow.

"Sounds like fun. Count me in. But I can't start until tonight." I had a plan to put into place. I batted my eyelashes and smiled widely to really sell it.

He only looked more amused. "Ah. Okay. Your booth

closes at six, right? How about we meet after that and discuss a plan for the week. That Chinese place you mentioned last night, around seven?"

"Oh no. It has to be *comida Mexicana*."

"Great. I love Mexican food. What's the restaurant called?"

"There are only five restaurants in this town. You really haven't spotted it yet?"

"No, actually, I . . ." He looked adorably flustered. "You know what? I'll find it. Seven it is."

Someone honked. I hadn't noticed the car behind him.

"Seven," I confirmed. "In the meantime, make sure you have a wet suit and hiking gear for the next few days. McCally's should have anything you need, but he's closed tomorrow for the—for an event, so you'll want to go today." I'd almost let the wedding slip.

"Closed on a Thursday?" When I nodded, he shrugged helplessly and muttered something under his breath that sounded like *small town*. "Perfect. See you tonight." He rolled up his window and waved as he drove away.

"See you tonight," I echoed even though he was already gone, a whirlwind of ideas filling my mind. I couldn't stop grinning at the possibilities.

This would be my best performance yet.

SIX

TANNER

Over the next four hours, I got no less than six texts from Jill, reminding me about the importance of this episode. Like I needed a reminder. Without Guy, my career would be fine. But he was the key to astronomical numbers, and he absolutely knew it. I had seconds to catch his attention with something different, something interesting.

Everything depended on Sophie, and she had no idea.

A little bell rang as I entered the sports shop Sophie recommended. The cashier, a blonde woman who looked fresh out of college, looked up and squinted at me in that you-look-familiar way most of my viewers did. She'd figure it out any second. I ducked under her gaze and made a beeline for the shoe wall, searching for a decent pair of hiking boots. As charming Huckleberry Creek was, it had a limited selection. At least what they featured here was good quality. I took a brown boot right off the rack and checked the size. Too small.

"I figured you'd go for the cleats, not hiking boots," the cashier said, leaning against the wall in a manner she probably thought nonchalant and casual. The excitement in her round eyes and the grin she couldn't hide revealed the truth. "I remember how much you love soccer."

I cringed. She'd definitely seen more than one episode, and likely in my Olivia days. "Not really my thing anymore. Knee problems. I'm going for a hike later. Do you have anything in a bigger size?"

She stepped closer, putting herself between me and the wall, and ignored my question. "Sounds fun! I'm Lucille, and I'm a big fan. Is someone taking you on that hike? I mean, is someone showing you around? Because I've lived here for six years." Her voice dropped meaningfully. "I can show you anything you want to see."

Wow. I looked around the store for help, but we were alone. Time to leave. "Actually, now that I think about it, my sneakers will do fine. It's a short hike."

"Why would you bother with a short hike when you can have a long one?" she asked. "There's so much forest out there with no one else around for miles."

Was this girl for real? I swallowed, tossed the boot onto a chair, and made a beeline for the double doors. "I'm good, thanks." I reached for the handle.

"Olivia was a fool, you know."

I paused, looking back at her. Not many people knew about Olivia. She'd appeared in a few of my episodes that first year, but people didn't realize how close we'd been. How I'd put a ring on her finger and a deposit on a house to surprise her. How I'd been hours away from signing away my channel when I took her to see our new house and how instead of being excited, she'd called it off.

Your vision for our future is obviously different from mine, she'd said. That was it. No other explanation, no apology. Not that I was all that surprised. Her soccer career always came first and I didn't expect that to change. But I secretly hoped she'd sprain an ankle and be out for a game or two. That I could compete with her dreams, or even be a factor in them.

But no. I'd been stuck with an empty house, an expensive diamond ring, and no reason to stay.

Putting down roots meant heartbreak. I knew that from watching my mom waste away in the same house, decade after decade, hoping my dad would come back. My attorney older brother, golden-child-Ben, had finally moved her into his basement so he and his wife could keep her company.

Mom claimed to be happy, but when I looked in her eyes, I still saw only pain. At least Dad could smile. He'd once told me that it was the *lack* of commitment, not a committed relationship, that brought him freedom and self-fulfillment and happiness—something I hadn't believed until the moment Olivia walked away.

So this would forever be my life, the flirty cashiers and fans following me around in sports cars with tinted windows, trying to figure out which hotel was mine. Collecting money that sat in a bank account with no end in sight.

Tanner Carmichael was free as a bird and liked it that way —because he already knew what the other path brought.

"Olivia wasn't the fool," I told Lucille. "I was." Then I pushed the doors open and strode back into the sunlight.

SEVEN

Sophie

I LEFT work early to beat Tanner to the restaurant. Sure enough, when I arrived and slid my jacket over the chair of my usual table, he was nowhere to be seen. I slipped into the back to find Mack bent over a pot of refried beans. The moment he saw me, his face split into a wide smile. "*Sofita*," he said in heavily accented English, dropping his spoon onto the counter to pull me into a hug. "You have stayed away too long."

"Sorry. Work has kept me busy."

He pulled away and clasped my shoulders. "How busy can you be? You are guarding a forest that's been there almost as long as the earth. It doesn't need you. *I* need you. Your *cemitas* are magic. Nobody else knows how to make them right."

"Yours would win any Texas competition in a second. Mine are barely worthy of the word." I glanced through the door's window, but Tanner was nowhere in sight. "Look, I need a favor. I'm meeting a guy here."

Mack stirred the bean mixture again, frowning. "To eat? I hoped you came to help. Daniel is sick tonight."

"I wish I could, truly. The thing is, there's a celebrity in town, and I need him to leave before he hurts anyone."

He whirled, his thick gray eyebrows shooting upward. "Hurts anyone?"

I could practically hear Carmen's chiding in my ear. *Don't be dramatic.* "Not physically hurt but just harming the town in general. He tends to bring the wrong kind of tourists, if you know what I mean."

"Mmm." He looked skeptical. "You want me to serve bad meat? Even if I had some, I don't think is right."

"No, no." If it got around town that I was trying to give the guy food poisoning, my plan would go kaput by morning. "Nothing like that. He just doesn't like spicy foods, so I thought you could give him a little extra kick. You know?"

His smile returned. "Extra kick. I see what you say now."

I gave him another quick hug. "You're a good friend. Thank you."

"I never want to be on your bad side, *muchacha*." He practically cackled as I darted back into the dining room just in time to see a red Tesla pull into the small parking lot.

Tanner must have run it through the car wash today because every other car in the lot, including mine, sported early-autumn mud. I kept my hands folded neatly on the table to keep from nervously touching my hair—which I had definitely curled for myself, not him—and pasted a smile on my face as he entered.

He searched the restaurant, his eyebrows lifting when he saw me. Okay, so maybe I'd put on a little makeup too. Fine, slightly more than a little. But tonight had to go perfectly. It was me against twenty million followers—surely worth an extra coat of lip gloss.

He sat and leaned forward, his hands folded. "Is there a

reason your Mexican restaurant is called McLaughlin's, or is that just to throw off the undesirables?"

My smile was real now. "Welcome to Huckleberry Creek."

He grumbled something under his breath, making me chuckle inwardly. One victory point for me.

He grabbed a menu. "So, what's good here? Tell me about your favorites."

I'd prepared for this question. "You have to try the beef flautas or the pork chimichanga, both with Mack's orange sauce. It's the secret ingredient."

"Done. I'll get both. Anything else?"

"Rudy's Rainbow Special Liquid Refreshment with no ice. Trust me."

"Sounds very Mexican." He chuckled.

When Mack arrived at our table with the menus, his eyes widened. "The travel man, sitting in my restaurant. What an honor."

Oops. Guess I should have warned him who the celebrity was.

Tanner reached out to fist-bump Mack. "Excited to try it out, *amigo*. Thanks for serving us today."

In a second, Mack seemed to gain control and cleared his throat. "What can I get you both?"

Tanner nodded to me to go first.

"We'll order drinks and food at once, if that's okay," I told Mack, who dipped his head in acknowledgment. The less time between drinking and eating, the better my plan would work. It also meant being here as short a time as possible.

Tanner waited for me to give my order, raising an eyebrow when I didn't order one of the meals I'd told him were my favorite. Mack scribbled away on his notepad. Then Tanner began with his order—in fluent Spanish.

Huh. Didn't expect that.

Mack looked up in surprise, grinned, then switched to Spanish as well. Within seconds, the two men were shooting the breeze like best friends.

Crap.

I strained but could still only recognize a word here and there—and they were words I'd learned in Mack's kitchen while filling in to help him out. Tanner said something with a chuckle, and Mack boomed a laugh. A moment later, Mack took our menus and waggled his eyebrows meaningfully at me as he left.

Well, crappedy-crapola. So much for my brilliant plan.

Tanner—one victory point. Tied up.

Tanner sat back, stretching one leg into the aisle in front of him. "Nice man. Interesting he closed a successful restaurant in Cancun to start again here. I don't know if I could have left those beaches for the harsh forestland of Montana."

Cancun? I'd known Mack since I could talk, yet he'd never told me about that. I fought the irritation brewing inside at having my friend stolen from me. "Let me guess. You're a surfing bum who prefers cute servers bringing him cocktails to the dangerous quiet of the Montana wilderness."

"Um, no." He coughed a laugh. "Pretty much every word of that is wrong. I tried to surf once, and it was a disaster, but my followers loved it. I'm not a cocktail person, either, and I may be here because this is where the dart landed, but I have to admit I'm also intrigued by your town." His voice grew quieter at the end, and he took me in with a sharp gaze—every inch, as if it were me, not Huckleberry Creek, that intrigued him.

I cleared my throat and found it surprisingly hard. "And you speak Spanish because?"

"I lived in South America for over a year, mostly Costa Rica. So, here's what I want to know. When I asked if you'd show me around town, you looked like you wanted to say no. Why?"

He looked genuinely curious. I had to be smart about this. I'd driven off Mr. 101 Questions last night with a series of lies, and Tanner saw through all of it, far too discerning for anything but the truth. But that was the one question I couldn't answer, not if my plan had the slightest chance of working. So I smiled sweetly. "My boss was standing right there. I didn't know if he would go for it."

"Interesting. The way you looked at him, it didn't seem like you liked him much. Actually, I could have sworn you hesitated for a different reason."

"Which is?"

"I've heard stories about small towns. Enough that I've been reluctant to visit one till now."

A defensiveness sprang to life inside my chest, and maybe a little relief too. If Tanner Carmichael was anything like Mr. Cuff Links, I'd have no guilt at all in driving him away. "Really? Do tell."

"I heard you folks are suspicious. Anti-progress, like those people who condemned the airplane as nothing more than a circus toy before it changed modern civilization."

Oh no. It was *on*. "Small-town 'folks' aren't grumpy old men defending their lawns. They're honest people trying to preserve a lifestyle they love." I clamped my mouth shut. I needed to be subtle for this to work.

To my relief, he nodded thoughtfully. "I can believe that. It really is charming here, and so are the people I've met so far." He pursed his lips as if remembering something, then seemed to decide not to mention it. "But I've found that people also get more superstitious in small towns. Did you hear about the huge resistance to boy wizard books in the nineties because people thought they taught witchcraft? Now look at how many of those children grew up to be voracious readers. I'm willing to bet very few of them actually became witches or wizards."

Those had been some of my favorite books, and my first inclination was to defend them. But then I saw the playful twinkle in his eye and knew he was baiting me. "A shame," I said. "The world could use a few more of those. Speaking of witches—the Huckleberry Creek Harvest Carnival is on Saturday, so you'll want to find a Halloween costume for that."

"The adults dress up too?"

"Every single one," I lied. "That's half the fun."

He gave me a pained look. "You'll be dressed up too?"

"Absolutely." I struggled to keep a straight face.

"I'll see what I can do." He released a long breath. "You know, I appreciate you doing this. You could have driven me away like your little friend last night, but you're giving me a chance. I won't make you regret it."

No guilt, I scolded myself. I simply nodded, unable to speak. No matter how sincere he seemed, he meant to exploit my town to further his career. I knew too much about men who showed up, took what they wanted, and then left us behind to clean up the mess. And I definitely knew how it felt to be used. No. What he intended to do was unforgivable. My plan was kinder than it needed to be under the circumstances.

"Tell me about your job," he said. "Alice told me you spend your days in that booth. You said earlier that you liked working there. Is that true?"

I hate it. "Of course. It's better than a desk job any day."

"What exactly does a forest ranger do? I admit I know very little about it."

"Most of what you'd expect. Finding tourists' kids who get lost, protecting and maintaining the trails, fire prevention. This time of year, we usually have an elk attack or two from visitors trying to take selfies with them. They don't realize that elk can be as heavy as a horse and punch a hole in a car door. We use paintball guns to keep them under control. It doesn't hurt them, but it's effective in keeping them away from humans." I felt another twinge of resentment. I was one of the best shots in the group, yet Paul had never allowed me to help with the rogue elk. Not once. "Don't get me started on the speeding cars. We lose several bears a year, some of which are moms leaving behind cubs we have to very carefully relocate."

"So you act like an advocate between nature and people, essentially."

"Basically. Although I wish we could evict the people altogether. The animals act better."

He didn't laugh at my joke. Instead, he studied me. "But don't you agree it's too beautiful to lock up and never set eyes on? People should see and enjoy it."

"I have no problem with the rule followers seeing it. It's the entitled ones I want to strangle on a regular basis."

"I see. Something tells me I'm going to enjoy seeing Huckleberry Creek through your eyes this week." He smiled—not in a judgmental way but in a truly curious way. "What's it like growing up in a small town and never going anywhere else?"

My head snapped up. "What makes you think I've never traveled?"

He raised his hands in surrender. "Sorry, you just seemed like the type that prefers home."

I shifted in my seat. This conversation had taken another uncomfortable turn. "My parents were from New York City. They moved here to run a boat store nearby."

"I can imagine they did well, then. I hear the lakes around here are postcard perfect. I haven't seen a boat shop around though. Did they close it and retire?"

Mack returned with two heaping trays of chips and a bowl

of salsa just in time to hear Tanner's question. He scowled. "Not a good subject for Sophita, *muchacho*."

As Mack set the food down and strode away, Tanner's mouth rounded into an O. "I'm sorry. It was clumsy of me to ask such personal questions."

"It's not a big deal. I just don't like talking about my parents."

"Then let's talk about anything else." He adjusted the phone sitting on the table, which I now saw recorded my every word. "Local birds? I'm guessing you don't have many flamingos here."

His joke made my frown quirk upward a bit, but the damage was done. "Not exactly. Let's talk about you. Why Costa Rica? I don't remember seeing an episode about your time there."

"It was the first place I ever traveled without my family, fresh out of high school. I spent the summer there with a friend and fell in love with the *Pura Vida*. After that, I couldn't stop exploring the world. I hopped from there to Nicaragua to Honduras to Guatemala and then Belize. Most Americans know about Cancun in Mexico, but there's so much to see and experience in those other countries. It's really remarkable how much history and culture exist that we live entire lifetimes knowing nothing about."

His words stirred something in my heart, an ache I'd buried long ago—a longing to explore the world and experience different cultures, different languages. Different perspectives and ways of thinking. Above all, seeing all the animals of the world and defending them in a way I couldn't do from a Forest Agency booth.

But my city-folk parents had converted to small-town life in a big way. When I came along, this entire town became my instant family. Each time I expressed a desire to go on vacation like my friends and see the world, Mom said exactly the opposite of what Tanner said—people lived entire lifetimes without truly exploring their homes and the people who lived nearby. That it was quality and depth, not quantity and breadth, that mattered. That we needed to see and appreciate every inch of this beautiful countryside before setting our sights elsewhere. It wasn't until I was seventeen that I realized her objections were rooted in fear and grief.

Then they'd decided to risk flying back to Manhattan to celebrate their twentieth anniversary—and never returned.

"Books can do the same thing, you know," I said softly. "Immerse you in other cultures."

"So does YouTube, except it's more accessible to youth. That's exactly why I'm here—to educate people who wouldn't know about any of this otherwise. My maternal grandparents were French, and my dad is second generation Italian-American, so my brother and I grew up surrounded by international culture." He shrugged. "I think I was always meant to travel. It's in my blood."

Then travel right on out of here, I wanted to say, but instead, I bit my lip. "That love of travel comes across in your videos. No wonder your subscribers like you."

He shoveled salsa onto a chip, took a bite, and nodded approvingly. "I do love my job. I don't love the trolls online, though. And I've had a few stalkers over the years. One woman guessed which city I was in, called all the hotels, and pretended to be my assistant so they'd give her my room number. She showed up at my door and said she was meant to be my cohost. Something about destiny."

I chuckled. "Let me guess—you didn't take her up on that incredible offer."

"Not exactly. She didn't like my answer. She actually went to the police and said I was stalking *her*. That was a fun week, let me tell you. I didn't end up doing a show there, and I hope to never go back."

So that's what it would take. Guilt stung me. I wanted him gone, but I would never stoop to such horrible tactics. "I had a homeless patron propose to me once. He tried to live high up in a tree. Built a treehouse and everything. Since it's federal land, we had to evict him and tear the treehouse down, which is a shame because it was pretty cool. I hear he's living in a shelter now."

"That's good. I'm guessing you didn't take him up on his offer either?"

"Sadly, no. Although I do have a thing for scraggly beards."

We laughed and fell into conversation about the ridiculous comments he'd gotten online and funny park tourist stories. This felt normal. Comfortable. Not as formal and uptight as a date but like two friends chatting. By the time Mack returned with our food, I'd almost forgotten about my plan.

The plate full of orange sauce brought that purpose front and center. My shoulders tensed as Tanner looked at his food and took a video of it with his fancy camera, which hung around his neck. I didn't even notice him bring it in. Then he brought a fork of chimichanga to his mouth. He closed his lips around it, chewed thoughtfully, and swallowed.

I gripped my fork and knife like they were about to save my life. Did Mack decide not to help me after all because he liked the guy? Maybe Tanner was used to hot food since he'd lived in South America for so long, and none of this would even matter.

But a second later, his eyes bulged. He swallowed again, his face turning red, and he grasped for his drink. I flinched as he gulped several swallows before choking and launching into a coughing fit. I reached out as if to help, then withdrew my hand.

"You okay, *muchacho*?" Mack asked. He hadn't left after

delivering our food. Maybe he wanted to see the stranger's reaction to the hottest sauce and spiciest drink in town. Or maybe he felt protective of the poor guy. Mack snapped his fingers and said, "Be right back" before trotting away.

The entire restaurant watched us now. Tanner's face turned beet red, borderline purple, and he couldn't stop coughing. I wanted to pound the guy on the back, but would that embarrass him further? He was a grown man, after all.

Moments later, Mack returned with a glass of milk and a plate of flour tortillas. "Try this. Bread is best, but I don't have."

Tanner waved a grateful hand, downed the milk, and shoved half a tortilla into his mouth. Then his shoulders slumped in relief. "Gracias, *amigo*."

"My pleasure." Mack gave me a stern look before stalking out.

"Not a fan of heat, eh?" I said weakly.

"Nah, I love heat." He coughed one more time and grabbed another tortilla. "Just not heat the size of Mount Everest. Man, that sauce would burn the hair right off a bear."

"Fur," I corrected. "Bears have fur."

He gave me a look I couldn't read. The restaurant had gone completely quiet listening to our conversation. He watched me, his gaze calculating, and I felt myself stiffen. This was where he realized I'd sabotaged him. He would stalk out like I'd done to my date the other night and never speak to me again. Some part of me, however little, disliked the thought.

But instead, he set down his fork, leaned back in his chair, and belted a laugh.

At that, the entire restaurant broke into laughter. I couldn't help but smile.

"We're two for two on restaurant scenes," he said. "Maybe we should avoid restaurants in the future."

"Probably a good plan. Are you all right?"

"The past twenty-four hours have been more fun than I can remember in a long time." He grinned and lifted his glass. "To making this week like none other."

I lifted my glass of Dr Pepper to meet his. The glasses clinked against one another in a way that felt official. "Absolutely unforgettable," I agreed.

♥ ♥ ♥ ♥ ♥

Carmen lay on the couch with a blanket tucked around her legs, gaping at me like I'd just announced an engagement. "You did *what*?"

"Don't you give me that look. It wasn't a date, just the first part of my evil plan to drive him from town." I dropped my purse by the door and slid my heels off.

She folded her arms, eyebrows raised. "I'm waiting."

With a sigh, I plopped myself down across from her. "Can't you just trust that I know what I'm doing?"

"No."

I swiped the remote from the cushion next to her hip, turned off the TV, and tossed it into her lap. "Fine, but I'm not explaining over your latest soap opera. I can't believe they still play this junk."

"It's *romantic* junk. You wouldn't know romance if it slapped you upside the head. Which I'm tempted to do, by the way. You met him for dinner and let him pay for you—again—and all you care about is getting him to leave? What's the matter with you?"

Once more, the old-fashioned Goodman stubbornness arose in my chest. "Someone has to defend this town. It won't be you or Mack or anyone else who's ogling him everywhere he sets foot. Just because he paid for dinner and has millions of followers doesn't mean he's a good person. He's ruining cities across America and doesn't even care."

"Ruining cities," she repeated slowly, as if trying to comprehend. "As in bringing them more tourism and boosting their economies?"

"We don't need more people. We need to protect what we already have."

She groaned and covered her face with her hands. "You're the most dramatic person I've ever met."

I wasn't in the mood to sit here and justify my actions. She didn't understand and never would, not when catching guys was her number-one objective at any given moment. I rose from the couch and strode to the kitchen.

She followed me and leaned against the doorway. "Look, I'm sorry. It's just that it's been ten years since your parents passed—"

"Not quite ten." It would be ten years on Tuesday, just a few days away—an anniversary that loomed constantly in my thoughts.

"Whatever. I've talked to people. I know you were the prankster of the town before the accident, full of dreams and jokes. You'd do anything to make someone smile. But you've changed even since I've known you. With each passing year, you spiral deeper into this place of solitude and sadness. I'm glad you find peace in the outdoors and the town you adore, but no forest can ever replace someone to love."

"I love plenty of people. I love Grammy, and you, and three-quarters of my neighbors, and most of my coworkers."

"That's not what I mean, and you know it." Her voice softened. "We love you right back, but Sophie, Grammy is right. You need companionship. It's been years since you dated somebody."

"There's nobody here I want to date."

"There's nobody here you'll let yourself date. But there are good men here, Sophie. And none of them are Alan."

"A good thing, because then I'd have to hide a body."

"And you know I'd help you. He was a jerk." She scowled.

No words could describe Alan. *Jerk* was an incredible understatement. "But I'm past him. I'm past everything. I'm happy, and my life is fine."

"Is it fine to invent imaginary battles with handsome strangers so you don't have to open your heart?"

I slammed the fridge closed. "You don't know what you're talking about." I brushed past her to my room, jerking away as her fingers tried to catch my arm.

I didn't slam my bedroom door—I wasn't *that* juvenile—but I did lock it with a loud click and turn up my playlist. One of my dad's favorites wafted through the air, upbeat and energetic. Everything I did not feel today. I swiped the phone from my pocket again and skipped the song, then the next, and the one after that. Finally, I switched to a different playlist altogether, settling on a sappy romantic song about a woman baring her heart and soul to a man she'd hurt.

How many times this week would I hurt Tanner before he left for good? Who would I have to become to win this?

I thought of my town again and steeled my resolve. The answer was simple: I'd become whoever I needed to become. Carmen called my struggle an imaginary battle, but she simply didn't understand. My trusting a stranger had already hurt them once. I would never let it happen again. Huckleberry Creek was my family now, and family defended one another.

I yanked a book from the tall TBR stack on my nightstand and opened it to a laminated turquoise bookmark a kindergartener had given me after last year's forest-safety presentation. There had to be fourteen books here, and I was partway through all of them. I couldn't even remember what this particular one was about. By the cover, it looked to be some kind of murder mystery.

Perfect. I hoped the victim's name was Alan.

Carmen's voice drowned out the words on the page. *No forest can ever replace someone to love.*

I tried unsuccessfully to immerse myself in the book and finally closed it to grab another. Carmen was wrong. The outdoors were everything she said—peace, solitude, an escape. But they were also a way of connecting with my parents that I couldn't find anywhere else. Surrounded by trees and brush and interrupted only by the occasional birdcall, I felt closer to them than ever. They'd chosen this place to be our home, and lately I understood exactly why.

My best friend had been searching for happiness in romance for the entire five years I'd known her, ever since her boutique chain sent her here to open and manage their newest location. In all that time, she'd only found temporary bursts of happiness with various men. She'd soon learn what I already knew—that a woman didn't need romance to be happy. Everything I needed lay right outside my door.

The music disappeared, and my phone vibrated. Grammy's face filled the screen.

I groaned again. I'd hoped she would miraculously forget about last night's Mr. Wife-List. A silly, pointless hope. If I let it go to voicemail, she'd just call until she reached me. I hit the green button and lifted it to my ear. "Hey, you."

"If you're going to ignore me, at least don't make your roommate worry."

"Let me guess. She tattled on me."

"No, she texted and said you could use a long-distance hug today. Besides, I wanted to tell you some good news. I'm coming into town on Sunday."

I sat up. "Really? Why?"

She didn't answer right away, and then I felt foolish for asking. I already knew the answer. Since I refused to fly and work wouldn't permit me more than a few days off at a time, the long drive to Florida was out of the question. So she was coming to spend Tuesday's anniversary with me instead.

"You don't need to do that," I told her.

"I want to. The humidity here is still unbearable. Besides, I need to check up on that cute house of yours, make sure your roommate hasn't turned it into a giant fruit salad."

That made me smile. Carmen had painted her bedroom and bathroom electric yellow, a color I detested. She would have painted the whole house if I'd let her. But this was her home, too, and I wanted her to be happy here.

"I did agree to let her paint the outside," I admitted. "It's bright, but at least we settled on green."

"Good girl. Now, are you going to tell me about this disaster of a date yesterday, or do I need to pry the details from your date himself?"

I flinched. "If you call him, I'm hiding under the bed forever."

"That sounds pretty bad."

"Worse than you think." I told her about the list in the guy's lap and my solution, deliberately leaving out any mention of Tanner.

She laughed for a full minute. "Sounds like I missed again, big time. I'm sorry, baby girl."

"It's all right. I appreciate the thought, but, like I keep telling Carmen, I don't need a man to be happy." The moment I said it, I mentally kicked myself. Grammy's husband died just months before my parents. How insensitive could one person be? "That was rude. I didn't mean that."

"Yes, you did. And I happen to think it's a healthy outlook, not needing someone else to bring you joy. I haven't been sending men your way to change or complete you, Sophie. I hope you know that."

"I do."

"Good. I only assumed you think about your parents as often as I do, and if that's true, you might be lonely. Just thought it might be good to have a little distraction during this anniversary. A handsome distraction. The richer, the better."

I chuckled. "Why rich?"

"So he can pay for your plane tickets to visit me, of course. You could do with a little beach time these days."

I felt my smile fade. "Thanks, but . . . I'm not boarding an airplane anytime soon."

"Of course. Silly me, forgetting something as important as that." She paused. "Well, we'll discuss a road trip, then. I bet Carmen would come with you if you bribe her with enough Mexican food."

Mexican food and two giggly women in the car on a two-day drive . . . now that *would* be an adventure to remember. My smile returned just slightly. But Grammy didn't get it. The outside world only held pain and danger. Huckleberry Creek was my haven, my fortress.

My parents resisted my pleas to travel the world for a reason. Turns out they were right all along.

"I'm excited to see you," I finally said, my voice tight, closing my eyes to shut out the image of Grammy's plane plummeting to the ground in a raging inferno.

"You too, baby girl. Don't worry. We'll get through this anniversary together."

EIGHT

TANNER

THE NEXT MORNING, I stood in front of a small house with a hand-painted sign that read "Huckleberry Creek Museum and Library."

"A museum," I said, feigning enthusiasm. "Great." I didn't love museums, and all my subscribers knew it. Anybody could go to a museum to learn about a place's history. If I meant to snag a contract with Guy, my episode would have to be different and unique. Fresh. Not a listing of dates and their accompanying black-and-white photos.

"This is the oldest house in Huckleberry Creek," Sophie said cheerfully. "I know how much you love history."

I'd never once said I liked history in my videos, but I'd chosen this woman to show me around. Time to trust her. "I've never seen a town museum that doubles as its library. How does that work—books interspersed with relics and old hunting rifles?"

There was a playful glint in her eye, one I was coming to know well. "You'll see" was all she said.

Turns out the house only had two rooms—what had obviously been the kitchen and living area and then a small bedroom that seemed to have been added later. There was no greeter, nobody at a desk demanding admission, just a glass jar with DONATIONS written on a label with a marker. Beneath it was a paper that said, "All books due within one month of checkout. No exceptions! Return one before you borrow another." Lines and dates with names scribbled next to book titles covered the rest of the page.

At least this town had its priorities straight, filling the bigger room with books. It held half a dozen metal shelves that felt far too modern for this space and contrasted the old spines in an intriguing way. It smelled like . . . old books. Old something.

Maybe just *old*.

I kind of loved it.

"The museum part is back here," Sophie said, heading for the addition, where I could now see a dozen pictures on the wall with glass cases beneath. But what grabbed my attention wasn't the museum portion—a book rested on the empty table in the middle of this room, propped up so it would be seen from the door. Several more copies of the same book sat stacked next to it, lined up neatly.

DEFENDING THE SMALL TOWN, the title read.

"By Trevor Goodman," I read. "A relative of yours?"

Sophie slowed, caught my line of sight, and flushed a brighter red than I'd ever seen. Clearly she hadn't meant for me to see this. "My father."

"May I?" I asked.

She nodded.

Her eyes followed my hands closely as I picked it up. Surely the town was proud of its author resident or they wouldn't have displayed it here like a trophy. I opened the pages and scanned to a section entitled "The People: Why They're Different."

"Cities like to make fun of small-town residents," I read aloud. "They consider them less educated, less wealthy or even downright poor, more easily entertained and manipulated, and generally rougher around the edges. You rarely see a politician or movie star rise from a small town. Why is that? Because they aren't worthy of international recognition or prominence? Not so. I submit they're worthier than anyone and among the most interesting people on the planet—and I would know."

I looked up to find Sophie staring at the book with a stricken expression.

I closed it and set it down, taking a few steps toward her before I remembered it wouldn't be appropriate to hug her. She was here in a professional capacity and seemed to want me to remember it. "I forgot you don't like discussing your parents. Are you all right?"

"I'm fine." If anything, her tone was angry, but not at me. More... bitter. "Come on, I wanted to show you what Huckleberry Creek looked like in its first decade. There's an early photo over here."

As interesting as that sounded—and it really did, strangely —it wasn't the mystery of Huckleberry Creek I wanted to unravel right now.

It was the mystery of Sophie.

I grabbed my camera and started recording as she talked, managing to get a few dozen clips of the town's artifacts. Since she hadn't given me permission to film her and stepped back so she wouldn't be in the shot, I respectfully kept my shots focused on what the museum offered. Sophie excused herself and went outside long before I'd finished. Despite the artifacts filling every spare inch, the room felt oddly empty without her.

When I emerged into the morning sunlight, Sophie knelt

on the sidewalk, eye level with a child wearing a backpack. The girl sniffled as if recovering from a good cry and rubbed her knee, which I now saw was bright pink. Sophie seemed to be comforting her. I stood back, careful not to disturb the moment.

"Some people kiss owies better," Sophie told her. "But you know what my mom always did when I hurt my knee? It's a family secret, so you can't tell."

The girl sniffed again and shook her head. "I won't."

"Good. Here's the secret: she would talk to my knee—lean right over and talk to it like it was a person. Isn't that silly?"

The girl grinned through her tears. "Yeah. What did she say?"

"She told it, 'Thank you for working hard so my Sophie can walk. And skin? You're doing a great job keeping the dirt and germs out. Sorry you're hurting right now, but I know you'll heal right up. I'll try to keep you protected till then.' She'd blow it a kiss and tell it goodbye and to have a good day. Then she'd look up at me and act startled, like she was surprised I was attached." Sophie chuckled to herself. "She always gave me a hug. Sometimes she'd also put a bandage on it and sometimes not, but it always felt better after that."

The girl wiped her nose on her sleeve and sniffed again. "Will you talk to my knee?"

"I would be honored. What's her name?"

The girl giggled. "My knee has a name?"

"Of course! They all do. Here." She leaned over the girl's knee. "Well, hello, beautiful knee. What's your name?" She cocked her head as if to listen, then nodded. "Interesting. Well, I appreciate your taking such good care of Kate here. I'm sure it hurts, but you'll start feeling better very soon. Have a great day, all right?"

The girl watched her in awe. "What did she say?"

"She said you already know her name. You just need to say it out loud."

The girl practically jumped up and down. "It's Sarah! I knew it!"

"Amazing," Sophie said, rising to her feet and sending me a knowing smile. "That's exactly what she told me. How did you know?"

I found myself chuckling. As the girl threw her arms around Sophie, I told her, "Have a great day at school, Kate and Sarah."

"We will!" She practically ran off down the sidewalk.

Sophie wiped her hands on her jeans as I approached. "Poor kid," she said. "It was a nasty fall. This section of sidewalk isn't the best in town." She cocked her head again. "What?"

I'd been staring at her in wonder. This entire scene just felt so different from Olivia, who'd never wanted children and barely glanced at them.

"Nothing," I told her. "Just thinking that was something special to watch." I wanted to ask if she loved kids, but I already knew the answer. I could see it in her eyes.

I'd seen her wear the same look talking to Mack last night. In fact, every time she talked to people, with the exception of the rude date from the other night, they left smiling. The woman certainly had a talent for connecting with people. And somehow she was single, or she wouldn't have been on a date with that guy in the first place. An odd jealousy hit me now, and it made no sense at all. He'd missed out on a huge opportunity. One I now wanted more than anything—the chance to go out with Sophie Goodman on an actual date with no business involved whatsoever.

Sophie wouldn't have walked away, leaving you alone with an empty house.

Not going there. Comparing Sophie to Oliva would only bring pain.

"Okay," Sophie said, her face flushed, and I realized I'd been staring at her an awfully long time. "Anyway, it's time for your tour of the town. You still need to see the school, the fire station, and the clinic. We don't have a hospital or I'd show you that too. Maybe the gas station and a couple of farms if you're feeling brave. My truck okay? It's a little loud, but the radio still works."

"I'd love it." To my surprise, it was true. None of what she'd said sounded particularly surprising or unexpected and definitely not the unique angle I'd hoped for. But anticipation shot through me at the thought of sitting alone with her for much of the day. Why, I couldn't say and didn't want to consider. "One condition—I'm buying lunch. Drive-thru this time."

She gave me a lopsided grin. "Wouldn't have it any other way."

NINE

Sophie

That night, I made a huge mistake. A colossal, monumental mistake.

I let Carmen dress me for a wedding.

"Oh, come on," she said with a chuckle, gesturing to my image in the full-length mirror on the back of my bedroom door. "It's not that bad. You look like a woman for once rather than a weapon-yielding forest soldier."

I pulled the dress's neckline higher to hide some of the cleavage I'd forgotten was there, and she batted my hands away.

"Don't touch it. It's perfect. Now, if only we can get Tanner there tonight to see you like this."

I turned on her and gave her the glower of the century. "Don't. You. Dare." I didn't like the mischievous gleam in her eye.

"Calm down. If Tess didn't invite him to the reception, it isn't my place. But a girl can dream, can't she?"

"Carmen, half the town is in love with him. Don't tell me he got to you too."

"Half the town is in love with him because they aren't as blind as you are, roomie." She slapped my butt like I was a horse or football player and slipped past me to open the door. "It's no crime to look, and you only have a few more days to do it before he leaves. So get a nice eyeful for the both of us." She grumbled something about her terrible work schedule before disappearing into her room.

I moved the door back to see my reflection in the full-length mirror again and instantly regretted it. At least Tanner wouldn't be coming tonight to get an eyeful of *this*. I wore a deep-orange sparkly gown that reminded me of pumpkin spice and fell all the way to the floor, a slit running up the entirety of the left leg. The bust fell far too low for my liking, making "the ladies" look awfully perky and full tonight. I also blamed the special bra Carmen let me borrow. A chain necklace hung down my chest and nestled between my breasts as if pointing downward in a very *Look right here!* kind of way. I reached behind my neck and unclasped it, carefully setting it on the bed. I'd tell Carmen I forgot it.

No more letting her dress you, Sophie. Never again.

I'd promised myself several times over the past year, yet I kept forgetting. It just made her so happy—and I could tell she missed the parties and social life of Portland. She appreciated the raise and the trust the boutique owner had in her, but choosing between Portland and a new job opportunity in a small town had been hard. Every day I walked into the kitchen and found her there, I was grateful for her choice. I couldn't even remember how or why we'd hit it off so completely given the fact we were complete opposites. I heaved a sigh of relief every time I arrived home from work, happy to get away from people. Then she would drag me out the door again, excited to be out of the shop's confining walls and see the people she'd spent all day missing.

"I'll be ready in ten minutes!" she called down the hallway.
"Can we take your truck? I'm almost out of gas."

"Of course." I made my way down the hallway, trying not to trip on the too-long gown, and grabbed a snack in the kitchen. I hadn't eaten since lunch. Which I'd eaten in the driver's seat of my truck with Tanner Carmichael, the YouTube star, sitting next to me. I wasn't sure I'd see the passenger seat the same way ever again.

Stop it. You are not starstruck by a guy you're trying to get rid of.

Our day had been packed with activity, exactly the way I wanted it—first with the museum, where I'd forgotten about Dad's book, and then the sidewalk where he stared at me like I was some alien creature as I talked to Kate Sherwin. I would never forget his expression. Haunted. Wistful. Pained. Then a tour of the town, where I'd rolled the windows down to enjoy the crisp autumn air. I'd caught him staring at me then, too, when he thought I wasn't paying attention. Worse, I'd found myself wanting to stare right back.

I still wasn't sure what to make of that.

Then I'd dropped him off at the hotel and told him I had work to do—which was true. My mother's best friend, Mariama, or Mari for short, needed extra help packaging the pastries for tonight's wedding reception. Since Paul had let me off for the week, it was the perfect opportunity. Tanner hadn't asked where I was headed when I dropped him off, and I wouldn't have told him if he had. The wedding was a town thing, an event for my friends. My family. He could see all the old buildings he wanted. Huckleberry Creek's buildings and structure were its skin and bones, the things most people saw when they drove through. Only a rare few saw its heart. I wanted to keep it that way.

When we arrived, Carmen's night-life friends instantly

swarmed her. At least, that's how I saw them—a group of reformed bar-hoppers who'd grown up in the city before creating their own little community here. I joined them on occasion to make Carmen happy, but I enjoyed the people-watching more than the companionship. Reading alone made me happier. And sitting quietly in my favorite spot on the overlook, which Tanner most definitely would *not* be seeing.

The wedding ceremony was beautiful—the autumn sunset seemed like a burst of fiery orange across the western sky, the perfect backdrop to Tess and Phillip's moment. Every chair held a smiling observer, and, to my delight, not a single one contained Tanner Carmichael.

The reception took place at the park across the street. Despite its commonplace location, Tess and her minions had worked their magic. White fabric floated overhead to form a massive extended tent. Fairy lights and potted trees and plants from Maddox's nursery added to the effect. Roger's quartet looked sharp in their suits as they played at the far end of the park, although the second violin was actually a flute and rather a rough one at that. It made me smile. I couldn't think of a better sound in the world. Several couples danced slowly in front of them, practically draped across one another as they swayed.

I paid my respects to the happy couple and looked for Carmen, who chatted animatedly with a man I didn't recognize. Must be one of the groom's friends. Phillip, Tess's new husband, had moved here only two years before to manage the sporting goods store and fallen for Tess long before she gave him a second glance. Love won in the end, though.

Carmen had mentioned several eligible men in the town. I skimmed the crowd, easily picking out several bachelors. I'd gone out with a few of them and avoided others. None gave me that feeling of magic, that thrill of something special being awakened in my heart. "The stirring that couldn't be denied," Dad called it in his book.

Was that my destiny, then? To wait for a handsome stranger to come to town and fulfill all my dreams?

I laughed out loud at the thought. My dreams. I didn't even know what those were. The last time I allowed myself to dream about a more fulfilling career, I chickened out before submitting my application. Leaving my town felt like betraying these people, turning my back on a family that embraced me. Needed me.

It felt like betraying my parents' last wish.

The crowd began to murmur, turning their heads toward the park entrance. I rose onto my toes and nearly stumbled in Carmen's heels. Were Tess and Phillip leaving early for their honeymoon? But the reception had just begun.

Carmen trotted over to me—a feat considering the uneven grass and the fact that her heels were inches higher than mine—and grabbed my arm. "Guess who just arrived!"

"He's so much hotter in person," one of her friends said, trailing her. "I think I hear angels singing. Birds are going to start falling from the sky any second."

Birds? I stared at her, but she seemed serious.

There was only one person who could make an entire town swoon at once. "If Tanner is here, he shouldn't be. I'll go talk to him."

Carmen grabbed my arm. "Don't make a scene. It's a wedding. The more, the merrier."

Then the crowd parted and Tanner appeared.

He wore a perfectly-tailored navy suit that brought the eye straight to his shoulders. It looked twice as expensive as any other suit here. Probably twice as expensive as any of our cars too. Heck, the groom had *rented* his suit for the wedding. Tanner's hair was slicked to the side with a few hairs brushing his forehead in a sexy, messy way. He'd even trimmed his facial hair slightly, leaving behind only a hint of dark stubble.

Tanner saw me and our gazes locked.

He stiffened and froze midstep, his mouth open, although nothing seemed to come out. His eyes combed me from top to bottom and back up again with eyes the size of the plates stacked on the refreshments table.

"Yesssss," Carmen breathed. "That's the reaction we're going for."

"You said you didn't invite him," I snapped.

"I didn't. But rumor is that Phillip did. Glad to see it's true."

I reined in my galloping heart and forced myself to breathe. Tanner had a string of women across the country—maybe even the world. He'd looked at dozens of women like this. Probably done far more than gape at them, truth be told. I would not be a part of his collection.

"I'm telling him to leave," I said and started forward.

"You are not," Carmen hissed from behind, but I had already crossed the dance floor to meet him. Tanner snapped his mouth shut, and his eyes grew guarded as I approached.

"What are you doing here?" I asked.

"Supporting the happy couple. You?"

"You don't even know them."

"Not true. I met Phillip this afternoon. The videographer said she could only do the ceremony so he asked me to get some footage of the reception. I was happy to help." He gestured to his camera, which I now saw was all set up on a tripod in the corner and aimed directly at us. "Say hi to the nice people."

I ignored it. "Phillip asked you to be the videographer?"

"Yes. Something about being on a tight budget?"

I laughed at that. I couldn't help it. Everyone knew Phillip was the cheapest man alive. He'd tried to convince Tess to get married at the courthouse and agree to a camping honeymoon—two ideas that did *not* fit Tess's bubbly personality. She certainly had her work cut out for her.

"So you come to make an episode for your channel and end up behind a camera at a wedding reception."

"Sophie, I had no other plans. I was happy to do it. Truly." He cocked his head, still gazing at me with an expression that sent tingles zipping down my legs. "You look absolutely stunning."

The sudden seriousness made me self-conscious. I wished I'd draped something over my chest, although he thankfully wasn't staring in a creepy sort of way. "Thanks. You too."

"No, really." His eyes crinkled with a smile. "I almost didn't recognize you without the can of bear spray."

In a moment, everything was back to normal. I felt my shoulders relax. "For events like this, I bring the fun-size can. It's less alarming to the other guests."

"If any bears come, I'm grateful we have you to protect us." The smile in his eyes finally reached his lips. The term "impossibly kissable" came to mind, though I couldn't say why. It didn't make sense and surely wasn't true.

Dozens of women, I reminded myself desperately. *Maybe hundreds.*

"Care to dance?" he asked, holding out a hand like Mr. Darcy at the ball.

I looked around in surprise to find that the music still played and people danced and chatted as if the entire world hadn't stopped for a full two minutes. I needed to get a grip on things, and quickly.

"What about the video?" I asked, glancing at his camera on the tripod.

"It'll record just fine by itself. I'll change the angle later." He still held out his hand.

I took it, ignoring the abrupt increase in happy zings shooting down my spine, and let him lead me to the dance floor —aka the wide-open patch of park grass. "Sure. Just to pass the time."

"Of course," he said, finding an empty spot and whirling me around to face him. "What other reason would there be?"

"None whatsoever."

He placed his hand on my waist and pulled me closer. I slid my hand from his and placed both my palms on his shoulders, feeling his other hand slide down to my waist in a way that made me shiver inside. The night felt hot and cold and somehow everything in between. Only a few inches of rapidly warming air stood between us now.

After a few beats, the music changed to an even slower song. Frank, the violinist, grinned and winked. Nearby, Carmen watched with wide eyes and a huge smile. *Focus on him*, she mouthed, motioning toward Tanner with her head.

I chuckled, bringing Tanner's attention to me without meaning to, and quickly pressed my lips together to hide a smile. How was I supposed to drive this guy away when the entire town seemed to be on his side?

Are you trying to drive him away? a little voice said inside. *Because it sure doesn't look like it.*

That made me pause. I'd shown him the mediocre parts of the town so far, hoping he'd get bored or think my town was too ordinary to hold his audience's attention. But that was a lie. Huckleberry Creek was a charming town full of charming people and history and secrets, and I couldn't pretend otherwise. Not without Tanner seeing right through my act like he had at the restaurant. The man was far too discerning for his own good. For either of us, really.

I snuck a peek and caught him staring at me, his lips lifted upward on one side in a kind of smirk I'd never seen him wear before. His gaze darted away the moment I caught him, but I felt my cheeks start to burn. I'd have words with Carmen later.

First Grammy and now my best friend . . . and apparently half the town. Clearly, I needed to up my game if I meant to win this battle.

"How is your video going so far?" I asked, careful to sound nonchalant.

"Fine. Lots of notes and general footage, but I haven't found a specific angle yet." He smiled again, the one he used in front of the camera this time. The extra distance put me slightly more at ease. "Remind me again what you have in store for tomorrow?"

I'd intended to take him on an easy hike to some popular falls near work, but that was exactly the kind of thing he wanted. I had to take this a step further. Run him out of town and find another group of victims to make him his millions. I would have to humiliate him—maybe hurt his manly pride a bit. And early, too, because he was notorious for being a night owl.

"The lake," I said with a grin. "Which means an early morning, so be sure to drink plenty of alcohol tonight so we can get footage of your epic hangover." For some reason, the thought of it made me laugh inside. I could completely see him stumbling around, his hair messy, his face full of dark stubble that felt rough against my hands—

Whoa. His hands on my hips, his fingertips brushing the spot of bare back the dress exposed clearly affected me more than I wanted to admit.

He grimaced at my words. Apparently he had experience with that scene. "I'll pass, thanks. Isn't it a little late in the season for a lake trip?"

"Most have winterized their boats, but I haven't yet. I like this time of year when the tourists are gone and I have the lake all to myself." That felt a little too genuine, so I pasted that fake smile on again. "You'll want to bring a wet suit, though. The water where we're going will be cold."

"Noted. I'll also bring breakfast."

I wasn't sure what kind of breakfast he could find so early, but I shrugged. "Deal. I'll text you the directions later."

"An address is fine."

I chuckled. "It's a dock, city boy. There's no address."

"Right." He didn't look at all abashed, smiling at me so openly and authentically I felt my earlier blush returning. His eyes didn't drop to my bust at all, instead remaining fixed on mine. From this close, I could see they weren't blue but a curious mix of sky blue and emerald-green flecks with an outside ring of brown. Three colors in one. A muddy mix of bright and dark and everything in between.

"Thank you," he said. There wasn't a hint of show about him now. His breath hit my skin, making it tingle again. "For showing me around. I have a feeling there are other things you'd rather do with your vacation time. Assuming you even want to be away from work. It seems like you enjoy it."

A dozen replies flitted to my mind, but it was something else entirely that came out. "I do like my job . . . mostly."

He cocked his head, pausing at the hesitant tone in my voice. "Mostly?"

"It isn't quite what I thought it would be."

Tanner's hand moved at my waist, finding more fabric again. My bare back missed where his fingers had been. "What did you think it would be?"

"Saving animals from humans, not the other way around. Preserving nature rather than helping destroy and alter it. Enjoying the world rather than trying to harness or regulate it." I clamped my mouth closed, surprised by my outburst. I hadn't even realized I felt this way about the Forest Agency. Why tell

Tanner, of all people, when I hadn't even told Grammy or Carmen?

He seemed to sense my inner struggle. "I get that. Being a YouTube star isn't all I thought it would be either."

"Not enough women falling at your feet?"

I regretted it the instant I said it. The warmth and honesty in his eyes closed off like a cloud over the sun, and his hand tightened around my waist. "Actually," he said, "I could do without that part."

The song changed to yet another slow song while we talked. I'd have to have a sharp conversation with Frank. Tanner looked around, taking in the tents and guests, and I got the feeling he was avoiding my gaze now.

"I'm sorry," I said honestly. "I'm sure that's a stereotype."

"It is. But one that fits, unfortunately. Or at least, it used to." His Adam's apple bobbed as he swallowed. "My subscribers like that aspect of my life, so we bring it out during editing. Most of the world knows I'm unattached and have been for a long time. I guess that makes me and my channel more desirable."

I wanted to point out that the tabloids had photos of him with a new woman at least every month, but that would make me sound like I was stalking him. Which I most definitely was not, even if I had binge-watched at least ten episodes yesterday alone. His face and voice now felt almost as familiar as that of my friends and family.

His hands on my waist, though—that felt new and utterly glorious. Electricity still hummed beneath my skin where he touched it, even through the thin fabric of my dress.

And he was staring at me again, I realized. Worse, I was staring at him. And we weren't moving anymore, just standing there on the dance floor while couples swayed around us pretending they weren't watching the YouTube star and his guide gaping at each other like they'd never seen the other before.

"I, um, need to go get a drink," I said just as he said, "I should check on the camera."

We both laughed awkwardly and separated. The instant we broke contact, my skin felt colder where his hands had been.

"Tomorrow," I told him.

"Tomorrow," he confirmed but didn't turn away yet. There was something wistful in his eyes, something deeper than the persona on his channel. Deep and beautifully complicated. Like a man seeing something he wanted but couldn't have—or, at least, wouldn't let himself have.

If Tanner Carmichael was as complex as his eyes, I was in serious trouble.

TEN

TANNER

Somewhere in the room, my phone buzzed.

I pried my eyes open and blinked away the fuzziness and confusion. The room was still black, preventing me from orienting myself. Where was I? Still in Wyoming in that mining town? I'd go back to sleep and figure it out in the morning. My phone said 5:00 a.m. Stupid phone.

Then I remembered. I was supposed to meet Sophie at the lake at six, and I'd promised to pick up breakfast. I already regretted agreeing to this.

Something still buzzed, but it wasn't my phone. Oh. The old-fashioned hotel alarm clock. I pressed every button I could find and still it buzzed. Finally I made a fist and pounded on the top. No luck.

I growled, slid to my feet, and unplugged it. Blessed silence at last. The past me had been smart to program that in addition to my phone, but now I wanted to take a hammer to everything in sight.

My phone buzzed again.

I nearly threw it through the closed window before seeing I

had a text from Sophie. *You sure you want to do this, Carmichael? Say no and we can both go back to bed.*

I grinned despite myself and texted back, my fingers fumbling in their haste to respond. *If you don't show, I'm stealing your boat and heading to Canada. I'll call you from Lethbridge.*

She answered quickly. *Sounds like we need a geography lesson. And, for the record, if you so much as touch Anastasia without me, I'm throwing you in. To the sharks. Which we totally have in Montana. I hear they especially love YouTube stars. Maybe something about being soft from all that traveling and restaurant food?*

I chuckled, wide awake now. She called her boat *Anastasia*, as in the Russian princess? I had to admit, Sophie certainly kept me on my toes. I typed my reply and hit send. *I've swum with sharks before, and they weren't all that interested. Kind of like the last girl I asked out, but that's another story. See you soon with some food.*

Scanning through what I'd just sent, I instantly regretted reminding her that she'd turned me down. Would it make today awkward? Would she decide not to show up if she thought I was coming on to her? We would be alone all day, after all. I didn't want her to feel unsafe or uncomfortable with someone who was essentially a stranger.

But my phone buzzed seconds later. *It isn't spaghetti, is it?*

I laughed, grateful she'd smoothed over my mistake. I could have ended the conversation there, but for some reason, I wanted to keep talking this way. Sometimes she felt so distant and distracted, keeping herself far from reach. I'd caught only glimpses of the real Sophie. But this conversation was the real her, and I liked this version more than I wanted to admit.

I waited a few seconds so I didn't seem too eager, then sent another reply. *You called it. I was going to bring you my famous spaghetti-flavored cappuccino, but if you don't appreciate it, I'll take my creation elsewhere.*

Sophie responded in less than a minute. *You'll find that I'm the most unappreciative person ever when it comes to pasta-flavored hot drinks. Maybe I'd better bring my own creation this time. Can I get you one? Something with plenty of jalapeños, perhaps?*

I belted out a laugh, feeling my respect level up another notch or two. The woman was fearless. *I'm good, thanks. I'm watching my jalapeño-coffee consumption these days.*

Pity, she wrote back. *See you at six.*

I read the entire conversation again, still chuckling, and headed for the shower.

♥ ♥ ♥ ♥ ♥

I arrived nearly ten minutes early, but she still beat me there. She sat against the morning light in the driver's seat of her boat—which did indeed read *Anastasia XVIII* in big block letters—wearing a white sweater and shorts that exposed plenty of her long, bare legs. Definitely not forest-ranger legs. Maybe fairy-dancing-ballet-in-the-forest legs. Her entire outfit contradicted itself, fall and summer, friendly and cold. Sophie would keep me guessing until the end of time.

Or until I left town in a few days, as I reminded myself yet again.

She watched as I set foot in the boat and plopped into the passenger seat next to her, which swiveled with a squeak. It had a tear on one corner with white stuffing poking out.

"I need to get that repaired," she said, handing me a muffin. I took it and handed her back the vanilla mocha latte the java cashier said she loved. I'd sat in the drive-thru for fifteen minutes waiting for them to open. This definitely wasn't LA with its twenty-four-hour Starbucks.

"Not a hint of pasta or sauce," I assured her. "Or even coffee, for that matter. I'm pretty sure they just lobbed a few scoops of cream in there and added hot water."

"Don't tell me you're the black-coffee type," she said, reaching over to pull the rope off the dock with one hand and holding her drink with the other. "Tough guy with his Tesla and straight bean juice."

"Wakes me up in more than one way." I sat back and sipped my own drink, feeling the hot liquid singe away the slight chill in the air. I'd worn board shorts and brought a backpack with my hoodie, good walking shoes, and a wet suit. I wasn't sure what this adventure would bring. This was Sophie, after all.

"It's too cold for lake sports," she yelled over the sound of the motor and the wind blowing past us. "But you've done all that."

"Right. I want to see what makes your town different."

"I'm not sure how different you'll find this, but it's something most tourists don't even know about. Certain times of the year, our destination gets cut off by water, and you can only access it by boat. That's not the case now, but I wanted you to see what it's like most of the time."

"Perfect."

Sophie must have felt my gaze still on her because she looked at me questioningly. I just grinned. She'd been breathtaking last night in her gown. But now? This was Sophie, her loose sweater flapping about in the wind and exposing a swimsuit strap and the gentle slope where her slender neck met her shoulders, her long hair flying behind her, sometimes whipping her right in her sharp brown eyes. Occasionally she'd lift a gentle hand to sweep it away, determination in her gaze as she steered us toward whatever adventure awaited. Behind her lay a stunning sunrise, painting the landscape in indescribable variations of pink, yet it couldn't hold a candle to this carefree woman sitting just inches from me, so independent and free and everything I wanted in my own life.

You're leaving in a few days, Tanner. Don't forget that.

I slid my sunglasses on, cutting off the warm colors, and took my camera out of its bag. I was almost sorry to put so many layers of glass between me and the view, but that was the way it had to be.

I turned on the camera and captured the moment for millions of other people to enjoy, careful to avoid filming Sophie. The magic quickly dissipated. In recording the moment, it was no longer ours.

Less than twenty minutes later, we pulled up to a rocky shore. She anchored the boat, giving *Anastasia* a pat as she powered down, then swept a backpack over her shoulder and jumped into the water to make the short trek to shore. She didn't even flinch at the waist-high water. "Coming?"

"Sure." I grabbed my pack and tried to slide in carefully. It didn't help. The water still stung like a million bee stings. "Kinda cold for September, isn't it? Seems like there'd be some of that summer heat left."

"This lake is too deep to heat much in the summer, and winter comes early here. Besides, if you think that's cold, you're in for a surprise." She grinned and marched up the rocky shore.

I tried not to let my eyes linger on the half-wet woman in shorts leading me toward the forest and followed, packing my gear over one shoulder.

The hike was less than five minutes. I knew where we were headed long before we arrived simply because of the sound of rushing water growing louder and louder. Soon, a fine mist sprayed the air, adding to the chill and making me forget about the dampness of everything below my waist. We rounded a bend in the trail and there it was—a tall, narrow waterfall spilling into a pool.

She tossed her backpack aside, slid her sweater off to expose a navy-blue tankini that nicely set off her brown hair and tanned skin, and slid into her wet suit. I did the same. Mine was a little tight, but at least it zipped up. I'd returned to the sports store after flirty girl left and guessed on the size. A minute later, Sophie climbed the slick black boulders next to the waterfall. I watched her a moment longer before realizing what she was about to do. Then a gnawing worry took hold.

"Are you sure about this?" I shouted over the roar of the water, eyeing the pool beneath. It was impossible to tell its depth. If she got herself paralyzed, what would I do? My phone didn't even have one bar to call for help. She didn't react to my question. I doubt my voice carried farther than my breath could. The sound of the waterfall drowned out everything else.

She reached the highest point and turned to face me, shouting something I couldn't hear. It was an impressive climb with ropes, let alone without them. She'd obviously done this many times. When I shrugged to indicate I couldn't hear her, she lifted her hands and pretended to hold a camera, using her finger to snap imaginary photos.

Interesting. She hadn't wanted clips of herself before, but now? I grabbed my camera and turned it on just in time for her to leap off, curl into a cannonball, and plunge deep into the pool, where she disappeared into the foam at the base of the falls.

Behind the camera, my heart pounded. Somewhere deep inside, I began counting. *One. Two. Three . . . Ten. Eleven. Twelve.*

Nothing.

I turned off the camera and shoved it into my bag before jogging toward the pool, staring at the spot where she'd disappeared. No movement.

That was it. She had to be putty at the bottom of the pool by now. I stepped into the water. The term "ice-cold" didn't begin to describe it. It felt like barely-melted glacier water. I'd brave it to save her life, though. A hundred times over. I took a deep breath and prepared to dive in.

She emerged with a gasp. "So refreshing!"

I gaped at her, feeling my shoulders collapse in relief. "Are you serious? I thought you drowned."

"No, I went to the bottom and sat for a while," she said casually, as if none of this were a big deal. "It's one of my favorite places—kinda dark and quiet but loud at the same time, like two opposites meeting in this weird middle place of neither and both and everything and nothing."

Was that supposed to make sense? "It didn't occur to you that I'd be freaking out up here?"

"No. Why would you do that?"

She looked perfectly innocent as I stammered, trying to find a response that wouldn't sound overprotective and creepy. Then she smiled. "I'm just kidding. Thank you for worrying about me."

"Yeah, well, please don't do that again."

"I don't need to. It's your turn."

"What?"

"It's . . . your . . . *turn*," she repeated slowly. "Do you need me to come with you?"

I gave an incredulous chuckle. Falling was a weird fear of mine. I wouldn't even cliff jump, something my subscribers constantly teased me about. "Funny. I'm not going up there. And if I do, I'm definitely not coming down like that."

Her lips scrunched into a cute pout. "But what about your

viewers? It's your duty to experience everything, is it not? You really think they want to see footage of me leaping down a waterfall and not you?"

I would watch that footage all day long, but that was beside the point. "This isn't my thing. I came to see the waterfall, not die in it."

"Don't be silly. Nobody's ever died." She paused. "Well, in this decade, anyway."

"Very funny."

She watched me expectantly, clearly not willing to move on and let this go. I refused to be seen as a coward in front of my own viewers. If Sophie jumped, they would expect me to jump too. She was right. But it looked pretty high from here, which meant it looked *really* high from up there.

"I'll film you," she said unhelpfully. "Do you want ropes? There are hooks if you need them."

"*If I need them*," I muttered under my breath. "No, I'm fine."

"Okay, if you're sure." She grinned wolfishly.

In that instant, I saw exactly what this was. She'd waged battle on that poor fool the first night. The next night, she'd tricked me into ordering the hottest possible dish. Yesterday she'd tried to keep me from the wedding—to stop me from getting to know the people she cared about, perhaps? And now she'd discovered my fear of heights, and I knew exactly how: episode 46, one she'd obviously seen, where my friend tried to push me off a cliff into the water and I fought tooth and nail, throwing him in instead.

This was no tour. This was a war. And at this moment, she thought she'd won yet another battle.

I returned her grin with one of my own. Tanner Carmichael didn't lose battles. Especially battles that involved cameras and beautiful women in wet suits.

I showed her how the camera worked, fastened my head camera and ran a quick test, then set to climbing. The rocks had plenty of handholds, but their being wet made the climb ten times harder. I scrambled up boulders twice my height near the top. It made me wonder how she'd done it when she was at least six inches shorter.

It seemed ages before I reached the point she'd leaped from. I turned to see her grinning from below—*far* below—and felt an impishness of my own. She'd practically dared me to match her jump. I would do better than that. I would beat it. I grabbed hold of the next boulder and pulled myself up, then up the next.

The grin on her face slipped a bit, then turned into a frown. She cupped her hands around her mouth, but I couldn't hear what she shouted. Her face looked genuinely worried. At least she cared enough for that. She could give the eulogy at my funeral. I could see the headline now: "Headstrong YouTuber dies on camera to win a silent battle against a woman he barely knows to preserve his manly pride."

Finally, the rocks were too smooth to climb any farther. I turned, gave her a salute, and stepped off the cliff.

The force of the falling water grabbed hold of me and *threw* me toward the pool. It felt like it was trying to rip my skin right off and flay me for the world to see. Despite its power, I felt suspended in midair for far too long, frozen by the frigid temperature and a very real sense that this was the stupidest thing I'd ever done—and I'd done a lot of stupid things.

I plunged under the water. Now I understood why it had taken Sophie so long to reach the surface—the combined power of the waterfall and gravity forced me down, down, and down until I wasn't sure I had breath enough to escape. Finally, I kicked outward and managed to get free long enough to swim upward toward the light.

She looked relieved when I broke the surface. In fact, she stared as I shook the water from my hair and approached, removing my head camera to toss it ashore.

When I stopped in front of her, I could tell she knew that I knew. There was a mixture of something I couldn't read in her eyes—relief, guilt, a hint of wariness.

I smirked and swept her into my arms.

"Hey!" she protested, but she giggled as I carried her toward the water. I'd intended to toss her gingerly, but she fought the instant I arrived at the water so I accidentally dumped her. She landed with a splash, sputtering and laughing. Then she kicked the back of my knee, forcing it to collapse, and wrapped her arms around my neck to pull me in too. I threw myself sideways so I wouldn't land on her. Then we were both sitting in the bitter-cold water, shivering and laughing at the impossible nature of this moment.

Before long, our laughter died and we sat there in silence despite the roaring of the waterfall. The world around us was quiet yet somehow not. Geese flew in formation overhead, their honking reaching us even over the noise of the waterfall.

"I've never seen anything more beautiful," I confessed. "I'm glad no tourists have found this place."

An insect buzzed past my ear, drawing my gaze to Sophie. She looked at me in wonder, like she didn't recognize this part of me. "You mean you aren't going to feature it?"

"It depends on the other footage I get. I may be able to persuade Jill to skip it. She understands the industry better than I do."

"Jill?" she asked, her voice tight. "Oh, that's nice."

"She's a bit of a pain, actually. And expensive. I swear she thinks I work for her and not the other way around. But she's one of the best assistants in the industry, so I keep her on."

"Your assistant. Right."

I gave her a sideways look. "Who did you think Jill was, exactly?"

"Nobody. I think this cold water has muddled my brain. Come on. I have something a little warmer to show you."

The next stop was a full twenty-minute hike, and not a casual one. I found myself scrambling over boulders and wishing I hadn't gotten so wet. But soon we reached another series of pools. I recognized the sulfuric smell immediately.

"Hot springs," I said, surprised. "I've been to the ones in Idaho but didn't know you had them so far east."

She slipped off her shoes. "Part of the same system, actually. Magma pockets heat the water underground for quite a distance. But this isn't like the ones in Idaho, so be careful."

I barely heard her as I undressed to my trunks and stepped in at the water's edge—where I recoiled immediately. "Wow. That's hot."

"Thank you," she said with a wink, suddenly sporting her swimsuit again. She strode past me into the water without flinching.

"You're kidding me."

"What, can't handle the heat?" she asked, settling herself down until the water was up to her neck. "You get used to it."

"There's hot, then there's sitting-in-a-volcano hot."

"Don't be silly. Lava can get past two thousand degrees Fahrenheit. This is only 106 degrees. You've sat in cars hotter than this on a summer afternoon."

"Not in my bare skin. Which I'd prefer to keep if you don't mind."

"I'm glad you don't sit in the car in your bare skin. That would be hard to explain to the people of Huckleberry Creek." She winked.

This woman couldn't possibly be for real. "It's not something I make a habit of, so don't worry." My foot still burned where I'd stepped in, yet she seemed mostly unaffected. "Fine, you've made your point. Are you sure you aren't some kind of heat-enduring Martian disguised as a forest ranger in Montana?"

"Montana, Mars. They sounded similar enough I thought this would be a good place to land." Her voice softened. "Turns out I was right."

There she was, up to her shoulders, and I couldn't even put my feet in. Gritting my teeth, I stepped in again—and felt like I was standing in flames. But I didn't recoil this time, waiting it out instead. Sure enough, I adjusted, and soon it didn't feel like fire and brimstone anymore.

I folded my arms and tried to look casual. "I can see how much you care about your town. You go soft when you talk about them, like they're your family. Not to mention your display at Alice's the other night."

Her face burned bright red now—whether from embarrassment or the heat, I couldn't tell. "I don't appreciate strangers insulting the people I care about."

I thought about her conversation with the girl on the sidewalk and the way everyone at the reception knew Sophie, smiling and relaxing the instant she greeted them. If she was like that with everyone, no wonder they all loved her.

She's easy to love.

I dismissed the thought before I could dwell on it much longer. "They're lucky to have a defender like you."

"I won't let anything happen to them." She lingered on the word *anything*, and although she avoided my gaze, I knew she'd intended it for me. I just wasn't sure what she meant by it.

As she stared at a nearby tree, I finally saw it in her eyes. The slightest glimpse, but a glimpse nonetheless.

Fear.

I took another step toward her, then another. Then I

gritted my teeth and sank in right beside her. She looked up at me with a mixture of respect and a rare vulnerability. This woman obviously fought an inward battle I couldn't begin to comprehend. For a moment, I wanted to remove whatever pain lay in her heart and let it dissipate into the open forest air.

"Tell me what this is about," I said.

"What do you mean?"

"You obviously don't feel comfortable with my being in town. I'd like to know why."

She sighed. "I'm not great at pretending, am I?"

"On the contrary. You're excellent. I, on the other hand, am terrible at reading people. It's something I need to work on. Unfortunately, that means I need you to explain." I nodded to her. "Please."

"It's not you, exactly," she said hesitantly. "It's your audience."

That was the last thing I'd expected her to say. The surprise distracted me from the stifling heat baking my insides. "I don't follow."

"But they do, and that's the problem. When you left Yakima, Washington, did you pay attention to what happened afterward?"

"I honestly have no idea what you're talking about."

"Your groupies took over the hotel you stayed at, terrorized the poor woman at the desk, and vandalized some vehicles in the parking lot. The guy who let you camp out in his field among the goats that one night? He had to hire security to protect his property because people kept trying to steal his animals simply because you petted them."

Oh yeah. The "goat camping" episode. "I feel for the guy, but I can't help what people do after they watch."

Anger burned in her eyes. "Reno, Nevada. A group tried to

race along the freeway at midnight to re-create your experience. Two cars hit each other and sent both drivers to the hospital."

That one I'd heard. The news made me sick at heart for days. "I lectured them about that at the beginning of the next episode."

"What about that skate park you visited in Milwaukee? The one with the teen who got hurt in that fight?"

Skate park? This was news to me. "Okay, but teens fight at those things all the time."

"Then there's the fire in Jamaica—"

"I get it," I said, putting my hands up in surrender. Jill handled my social media accounts, and I rarely watched the news, so maybe I needed to change that. "Wait. Did you say there was a fire?"

She smiled grimly. "Just over half of Huckleberry Creek's residents once lived in big cities. They came because, here, we take care of each other. We protect one another. We can't keep bad things from happening, but some of the worst disasters hit when some of us left the safety of Huckleberry Creek for out there," she said, waving past the trees, "or when an outsider brought danger to us. Maybe not intentionally, but their fault nonetheless."

It all came together now. "You think my followers will descend on your town and hurt people."

"They've done it everywhere else. Why not here?"

"You believe that driving me away before I can expose this town will keep you safe." I cocked my head, suddenly seeing her in a new light. "You aren't the grumpy old man defending his lawn. You're the mama bear protecting her cubs. The question is, why do you feel so responsible for them?"

She put her face in her hands as if embarrassed. I'd hit some kind of nerve, I guess, because she sat like that for a long time. A trickle of sweat ran down my neck as I waited.

"It's time to leave," she finally said, finality in her voice.

I groaned inwardly. "I appreciate how much you love your town, but I really think we can work this out. If I give some kind of disclaimer—"

"No, I mean I need to get out. I feel dizzy." She dropped her hands. Her face looked redder than before, her gaze distant.

Then her eyes rolled back into her head and she collapsed into the water.

ELEVEN

Sophie

A headache loomed behind my eyes like a distant storm. Above me, a shadow blocked the sunlight. Trees? And a face. I really liked that face.

The face sighed in relief. "You scared me, Sophie Goodman. I thought I'd have to summon those old lifeguarding skills from high school."

No, no. I did not like that face. Or I did but wasn't supposed to?

It took a moment to remember what happened and who he was, this shirtless man sitting on the ground with my head in his lap. And I most definitely did *not* stare at the hardened chest only inches from my face.

Sophie, pull it together. He'd just made a joke about lifeguarding. I tried to recall his words. "Oh, dear," I managed. "I wouldn't have survived that."

"Truth. I don't remember much from those years. Mostly that Mr. Rothburt picked his nose when he thought we weren't watching."

I sat up, my full memory returning. "I fainted?" Oh no. He must have carried me to shore and stretched me out here, fully unconscious. Panic swept through me as strongly as the sudden dizziness.

"I—I'm sorry," I said. "Not sure what happened there. I've come here a hundred times and never had a problem." Of course, I usually got out within ten minutes. Who knew how long we'd been talking? "I'm so embarrassed. Thank you for . . . for saving me." I had to drag that last part out.

I despised feeling like a damsel in distress. So much.

"Look," Tanner said, smiling with a warmth in his gaze I hadn't seen before. "You want to keep your friends safe, and I respect that. And I haven't chatted with many Huckleberrians yet. But there's one thing I absolutely know is true." He brushed a piece of ratted, limp hair out of my eyes, sending a different kind of heat across my skin. "The ones I've gotten to know so far are definitely worth protecting."

♥♥♥♥♥

Things were . . . not going well.

I still lay in bed with my PJs on despite the bright late-morning sunlight bursting through the blinds, staring at the ceiling that clearly needed a fresh coat of paint. Every time I thought about yesterday, I wanted to kick myself. *Way to go, Sophie.* I came so close to getting through to him and then my body failed me spectacularly, erasing all my progress. If anything, I gave Tanner the impression that we wanted him here. That I *needed* him.

And then I thought about yesterday again, and my stomach

soared to the sky. For hours after the hot-springs incident, he'd watched me with such concern, such care, that it melted something inside of me I thought forever frozen. Or maybe that was just the hot springs trying to melt my guts. He'd even texted me five times since dropping me off, urging me to see a doctor to make sure I was okay. My quick call to Doc Susan finally gave him peace of mind. There was already a text at 8:00 a.m. this morning to check in. I hadn't answered. Physically, I felt fine. Mentally? Emotionally? I was a disaster.

He'd saved me. Plucked me right from the water and carried me around like some victorious hero, the helpless princess draped in his arms. I imagined those arms cradling my unconscious body, his watchful gaze on me while he prepared to give me CPR. If I'd stopped breathing, he would have leaned over and placed his beautiful mouth on mine—

Wow, Sophie. Get a grip.

I felt humiliated and elated at the same time, two parts of myself at war inside. I never wanted to see him again. I wanted to see him again right this second, to experience his touch once more but awake so I could remember how it felt. I wanted to pretend it never happened. I wanted to tell the entire world.

I smashed the latter voice down and banished it to the far ends of the wilderness. Romance had no part of my life right now and definitely not one with a YouTube star who hadn't lived more than a week of his adult life in the same place. He exploited a city and then moved on without caring what would happen afterward. I knew this. He hadn't even denied it.

And yet.

I shook my head to clear it and swung my legs over the edge of the bed. The events of yesterday changed nothing. Tanner seemed determined to continue with his episode, which meant helping him see reason wouldn't work. There was a lot to be done in preparation for the harvest carnival this evening. After yesterday's disaster, tonight had to go perfectly.

Meaning, of course, that it had to go as imperfectly as possible.

♥ ♥ ♥ ♥ ♥

The harvest carnival was already packed by the time I arrived. I'd planned it that way—longer lines meant more frustration. But long lines weren't going to deter Tanner Carmichael. No, I had bigger plans than that. I waited on the curb of the parking lot as he pulled up and slid out of his car. I braced myself for the conversation I knew would come when he discovered I'd tricked him about the costumes, but he was nothing but smiles when he saw me—and also dressed in black from head to toe, leather jacket and all. He carried a plastic bag in one hand and his camera case in the other. It took me a second.

"Danny Zuko," I said with a chuckle when he reached me. "Nice. Grease is always a good choice."

"I'm glad you think so because I figured you'd 'accidentally forget' to dress up, and I brought a little something to ensure I wasn't alone." He set his case down and opened the bag for me to peer inside.

I snorted. "I am *not* wearing tight leather pants."

"It's only fair. I'm melting inside this jacket."

I opened my mouth to tell him it looked hot, too, and he should leave it in the car, but I thought about the double meaning and snapped my jaw closed.

"I'll wear it," a voice called out.

We turned to find Lucille striding toward us, her blonde waves bouncing over her shoulders.

Tanner closed the bag. "It was just a joke. Don't worry about it."

"No, no," Lucille said, taking the bag with pristine baby-yellow fingernails. She flashed him a brilliant smile. "Don't be silly. Danny can't go to the Huckleberry Creek Harvest Carnival without Sandy. It's in the rules."

"Is it, now?" Tanner looked hesitantly back at me. "I guess—"

I yanked the bag from Lucille's hands as she gave a petite, startled yelp. "I'll wear the stupid pants." Then I strode toward the restrooms, Tanner's chuckle following me all the way.

A few minutes later, I emerged to find Lucille and Tanner engaged in conversation, her hands moving animatedly. He laughed at something she said—not the fake, scripted one from his show but a genuine one—the type he offered me when we were alone. The sound pierced me like a lightning bolt. I found myself slowing to stare at them, my gut stirring with something that felt an awful lot like hurt.

When his gaze lifted and he found me, his smile widened. "There she is. Looks like they fit."

"In a manner of speaking." They squeaked when I walked, and I felt like I couldn't stride as deeply as usual, but I felt like Sandy. Now I just needed a tight black shirt that showed off my shoulders and we'd be the cheesiest couple here. The thought warmed me from head to heel. I offered an elbow. "Shall we?"

"I'd love to." He took it, nodded a farewell to a huffing Lucille, and turned his full attention to me. I'd just lost the battle to Tanner, yet I felt I'd won something far greater.

Or maybe *someone*.

We walked toward the crowds gathered around the food

trucks and three carnival rides set up near the center of the park. It was a completely different scene from two days ago when I danced with him near this spot and felt the world around us freeze in time. Food trucks lined the lawn, the old trees dropped their bright yellow and orange leaves, and a stack of pumpkins towered over the Pumpkin Walk, where a circle of children in costumes leaped from number to number. The smell of fresh-baked pies from one of the stands made my stomach rumble despite the fact that I'd just eaten. A chorus of young, delighted screams rose from the "Haunted" Trailer at the far end of the row. Its doors hung wide open, held in place with straw bales topped with grinning jack-o-lanterns.

Tanner had extended his elbow for me to take, and we now matched our strides, arm in arm. Whispers peppered the crowd around us as people turned to stare.

He seemed oblivious as he looked around, smiling. "Small-town carnivals are so charming. Do they have that spinny ride that's super questionable?"

I motioned toward the ride that looked like an alien spaceship with colorful lights. "Of course. What's a carnival without a questionable ride or two?"

"Agreed. The dinosaur thing is new though." He nodded toward Benny the Brontosaurus, a plastic dinosaur big enough to ride and who currently wore a fur coat and baseball cap and smiled at newcomers entering the park. "Any special meaning there?"

"Now, that I can't tell you. You'll have to guess."

"The god of the Huckleberry Creek harvest."

"Sorry, that's a big black bear."

"Of course it is." He frowned thoughtfully. "Then it must be a gift of peace from a neighboring town."

"Not quite."

"A graduation gift? We bought a big rubber spider and gave it to the principal. She didn't appreciate it much."

I couldn't help it. I laughed. "No, but that's good to know. I'll be sure to look out for giant rubber spiders."

"Then there's only one other thing it can be—a monument to the town's founder in the 1800s." He pumped his free arm to the sky. "Thank you very much, ladies and gentlemen."

"You're pretty close, actually," I admitted. "It's an old gas-station gimmick that got moved here when it shut down. Benny's become the town mascot. The mayor even tried to have him put on our 'Welcome' billboard, but nobody could agree on where he should be permanently placed. So now Benny gets moved around. Sometimes you'll find him outside the library, sometimes in the grocery store parking lot. He even showed up in the yard of a family who had a new baby. They came home from the hospital and there he was, guarding their house wearing a giant diaper."

He chuckled. "Now *that* is going into the show." He began to set up his tripod.

I felt my smile die and reminded myself for the hundredth time that I was driving him away, not convincing him about the charming nature of my town . . . and myself. And I certainly wasn't trying to make him feel welcome here. I looked around and saw a group of church ladies—mostly single and a couple who obviously wished they were —approaching.

"Here comes the cavalry," Tanner muttered.

Just then, I caught a glimpse of Nate under a tree. "I'll be right back."

Tanner looked at me in mock horror. "You're throwing me to the wolves?"

I just winked as the church ladies swarmed him, not like a pack of wolves as much as a hive of bees, all circling him while a few reached out to touch his arm, chattering away. He shot me a helpless look as I left, chuckling to myself.

By the time I reached Nate, his mom was pushing his wheelchair toward the shaved-ice truck. Smiling at me, she bent down to whisper in his ear as I approached. My little friend's face lit up. "Sophie!"

"Hey, buddy. I haven't seen you in a while. What have you been up to?"

"Physical therapy in Missoula. Mom found some specialist there that's helping with my hands. Right, Mom?"

She nodded and put a hand on her son's shoulder. "School has been hard for him. There aren't enough resources available to get him the assistance he needs. If I didn't have to work . . . anyway, the specialist works with tetraplegic patients who have partial paralysis in their hands. The therapy's intense, but Nate's handling it beautifully. Aren't you, big guy?"

"That's what everyone says." As usual, Nate sat stock-still as he spoke. I'd gotten used to it, but occasionally, the memory would return of what he'd been like before, running around playing football in this very park and riding his bike on the sidewalk. It brought back a familiar pain in my chest, a pain that would never go away.

"And I heard you're getting a new wheelchair," I said, swallowing back the emotions.

"Yes! For Christmas. It'll be so much better than my old one that broke. Then Mom won't have to push me around everywhere."

"I don't mind, silly," his mom said.

"But I do. You only want to talk to old people and always about boring stuff." He rolled his eyes.

I put my hands on my hips and laughed. "Old people like me?"

"You aren't old. You're my friend."

I gave him a brief hug. "Why, thank you. So, about that shaved ice. Which flavor will it be tonight?"

His face brightened. "Cherry and grape with a dab of blue raspberry."

I playfully rubbed the top of his head. "I thought you liked weird combinations. Those aren't weird."

"They are when you mix them. They turn into this oozy brown mess. And they taste good together. You want one?"

"I'm not a fan of cold treats," I told him. "I have sensitive teeth. You'll have to enjoy it for the both of us."

"Good thing I brought this, then," Tanner said, coming up behind me with two lidded cups. He handed me one. "Hot cocoa for the lady. Extra cream. Not sure if there's anything *besides* cream in there, to be honest."

"Then it's made right." I placed both hands around it, letting the hot cup warm my chilled hands. Despite the sun setting earlier and autumn in full swing around me, I kept forgetting how cold it got at night in the fall.

Nate's eyes couldn't be wider. "You're Tanner from *Tanner Carmichael Travels the World!*"

Tanner leaned over to look Nate in the eye. "Indeed. Who might you be?"

"Nate Stewart. I watch your show all the time. Just ask my mom."

His mother laughed. "He isn't lying. He wants to travel the world too—as soon as he turns eighteen in seven years." Her eyes grew slightly misty at that, but she quickly reined it in. Even after high school graduation, Nate's travels would require a companion to help.

The sight of his mom's emotions surfacing, even for the briefest of moments, made that familiar pain stab through my chest again.

"There's a lot to see in this world," Tanner said. "If you want, I'll make you a list of my top ten favorite places."

"Really?" Nate asked, his voice full of awe.

"Of course. It would be a waste to stay in the same place your entire life if you don't want to."

Being here is such a waste, Mom. I want to see the world too. My own words, said at age seventeen. In a moment, the memory came flooding back.

She'd been packing for their trip. Since they'd never left town before, and especially since they hadn't left *me* behind before, I felt a little betrayed. It was their anniversary trip, so obviously I didn't expect them to bring me along. But Mom seemed more open to the idea of traveling than she'd ever been, so I saw the moment as my opportunity to negotiate a future trip for the three of us. She'd stamped out the idea immediately.

"But why?" I'd shot back. "Being here is such a waste, Mom. I want to see the world too."

She could have gotten angry, but she didn't. Instead, she stopped packing her suitcase and came around the bed to sit next to me. "Maybe someday you will. But right now, it's comforting for us to know you're safe in a town full of people who love you."

I hadn't known it would be my last real conversation with her. One moment my parents were there, large as life, waving from the car window. The next, they were gone forever.

And Nate had almost followed not too long ago.

Suddenly, I didn't want Tanner anywhere near my little friend. "Nate, I have to take Tanner away for a while. I'm showing him the cemetery tonight."

"Ooh! Will you show him the shoe stone? That's my favorite."

"Of course."

He turned back to Tanner and waved. "Nice to meet you."

"You too, buddy."

Seeing Tanner acting so cute with Nate hurt even worse. I couldn't get away fast enough. In fact, Tanner had to jog to catch up. He'd hurriedly packed his tripod and camera, I noticed, as only two of the clasps on his suitcase were fastened. A hurry to leave the group of women or a hurry to overhear my conversation with Nate?

"What a special kid," he said, matching my stride. "Why do I get the feeling you didn't want me talking to him?"

"Nate is off-limits," I said curtly.

"Can I ask why?"

"No."

He blinked at my sharpness, looking stung. But this wasn't something I could explain. Not with words, not with pure emotion. My heart was still working out the details, and I wasn't sure I'd ever completely unravel what happened.

The walk toward the cemetery entrance was a quiet one. I caught him glancing at me a few times, but I didn't return his gaze. I couldn't. My thoughts were locked in an iron grip of regret and hurt, a place I rarely escaped from unscathed. The only consolation lay before us as we stopped at the iron arch entrance. There, displayed in all its glory, a brilliant orange-and-purple sunset awaited.

"Wow," Tanner breathed. "Even your sunsets are better here." When I didn't answer, he turned to me with a somber expression. "You've done so much to help me the past few days. I want to help you, but I'll admit I feel utterly helpless to do it."

"It's not something you can help with." I left the rest unspoken: *Especially when you're leaving in a few days.* "You should get a shot of this."

He watched me for a moment longer while I tried to ignore him. His gaze felt like a giant spotlight trying to burn through my eyeballs to my brain, piecing together everything that lay beneath the surface. Then he finally grabbed his camera and filmed the sky until the sun dipped past the horizon, plunging the world around us into gray.

He hung the camera around his neck and motioned to the cemetery before us. "I'm fascinated by graveyards. They tell the stories of the people who lived there better than anything I know. If you have any interesting stories, I'd love to hear them."

I'd intended to sabotage Tanner tonight like never before —take him on the dizzy and nauseating rides, allow him to get swarmed, and make him as uncomfortable as possible. But now I saw how childish my behavior had been. Especially now that he knew what I'd been trying to do . . . and was somehow still here, seeming to enjoy my company. The harder I pushed him away, the sweeter and more attentive he got.

It was infuriating.

My heart pounded like I'd just run a race even though we'd done nothing but stand here. "Nate wanted me to show you the children's section. He likes the stone with the baby shoes. But I . . . I can't. Not right now." Some tiny part of me wanted to toss all my plans aside and take Tanner to the farthest edge of the cemetery where a joint headstone with my parents' names stood. But the rest of me—the smart part—wanted him as far from that as possible. I was such a mess.

"Take whatever time you need. We can even go back to the carnival if you want." His fingers slid down my arm, sending a wave of delighted shock through me, and he took my hand.

Took my hand.

And held it firmly.

Something deep inside screamed at me as if with a hundred wailing fire-truck sirens. *Danger. I've been here before.* But I couldn't get myself to tear my hand away, not when it felt so warm and kind and, oddly, eased some of the pain in my heart.

"No," I finally said, my voice suddenly hoarse. "If it's stories you want, I have one to show you. It isn't far."

I took him around the corner, two blocks away. His hand gripped mine all the while, our arms brushing on occasion. Each time, I wished his arm would slide around my shoulders and pull me close to his chest. I wanted him to envelop me in every way possible, to form a wall between me and the pain, to hold me until the pain dissipated and there was just him.

This time, I didn't shove the feeling away. I squeezed his hand. He immediately squeezed back.

I pulled him to a stop in front of a little blue house with a picket fence. It looked gray and ominous in the darkness, no different from those surrounding it, its age indicated more by the thick trees in front than anything. I brought him up the narrow driveway to the side of the yard where we could see the shadowed barn in the backyard.

Tanner watched me curiously, waiting. Something told me he would wait all night if necessary.

"To date," I began, "every citizen of Huckleberry Creek has been laid to rest in the cemetery upon their death except for one. The man who built this house was a night watchman in the early 1900s. While patrolling the cemetery, he caught a group stealing from a new grave and drove them off. He declared that he'd never been a victim of theft in his life and he certainly wouldn't be upon his death. His dying wish was to be buried in that barn, with the key destroyed and the barn's entrance sealed. That way nobody could steal from him."

I expected Tanner to look disgusted, but he only appeared intrigued as he stared at the barn. "Is he still there?"

"No. The fourth set of owners got fed up and had his coffin moved to the cemetery. But the coffin's lid shifted during transit and they realized the lock had been broken a long time ago. Seems somebody saw his precautions as a challenge and took what they wanted anyway. Whoever it was is likely long dead." I shrugged.

"I can't imagine living with a rotting corpse in my backyard," Tanner said, still gazing at the barn. "I'd have him moved too."

"I wouldn't."

He turned to me in surprise. "You'd leave him there?"

"If that was his dying wish, yes. I think people's last requests should be respected."

"But that isn't him anymore. It's a box of bones. The people who own the barn should have a say too."

"It's a burial place. It's sacred. Untouchable."

He pursed his lips. "But for how long? Some of his great-grandchildren have likely passed by now."

"And they should be upholding his legacy more than anyone," I snapped. "It's how we honor the people who lived before us, following through with what they wanted—for their sakes and ours alike."

He stared at me for a long moment. "This isn't really about the dead guy in the barn, is it?"

I didn't know anymore. I slid my hand from his, turned, and walked back toward the carnival. A couple of minutes later, I heard his footsteps following at a respectful distance. I think he could tell I didn't want to talk just then, but I also detected a frustration that meant he had a lot of unanswered questions. I just wasn't sure I had any of the answers he wanted.

When we reached the park, I kept walking to my car and unlocked it.

"Sophie," he said, reaching me at last. "If I said something offensive or hurtful—"

"You didn't. I hope you got the footage you needed."

For the second time that week, I pulled out and drove away, looking back only once to see him standing there, watching.

Nothing had changed since that first time. Yet, somehow, everything had.

I brushed a tear aside so I could see clearly to drive. In three days, it would be ten years since I said goodbye to my parents for the last time.

A decade, yet the pain sometimes came back so strongly I couldn't breathe.

TWELVE

TANNER

What just happened? In utter confusion, I watched Sophie drive off. Again.

Trying to distract myself by taking more video footage of the carnival only made me frustrated. I saw her in everything and felt her absence everywhere. After the tenth conversation with a fan who asked where Sophie had gone off to, I climbed into my car and sank into the seat, replaying our conversation in my mind. My brain couldn't pick out a single word that could have set her off like that. Women were strange creatures.

I drove to the grocery store and slipped in just before it closed for the night. It would take a while to get used to the hours of small-town businesses.

You're leaving soon, remember? Your next stop is Columbus, Ohio, where you'll start all over again. Just like always.

The thought made me sad. I couldn't leave Sophie like this, clearly upset. The only appropriate goodbye would be to take her into my arms and . . .

Whoa, cowboy. Not going there.

A woman dressed in yoga pants and a heavy hoodie slid

through the closing automatic doors and made a beeline for the frozen section in the far back. A twinge of a dark braid escaped her hood. It looked familiar.

"Wait!" I called after her, but she sprinted away down the bread aisle.

I turned down the next aisle and ran to head her off, getting a startled look from a father with a wailing toddler. Sophie's roommate, Carmen, stood right where I'd guessed she would be —in front of the ice cream section.

"I need to talk to you," I said.

She turned to look at me, her eyes narrowed in suspicion. "Not until I get an explanation."

I slid a hand behind my neck, feeling more baffled than ever. "I was hoping you could give me one. One minute we were talking, and the next she was driving away. Is she all right?"

"She'll be fine once I get some . . ." She looked at the carton in her hand. "Elk tracks with extra chocolate into her system."

"Here," I said, grabbing a glass bottle of fudge off an end cap and handing it to her. "Maybe this will help."

She took it warily. "At least tell me how your conversation went? She won't say a thing."

I tried to think. "I met Nate, but she wouldn't let me talk to him very long, and then she was really quiet when we went to the cemetery."

Carmen sighed, letting her shoulders slump. "I should've figured seeing Nate would set her off. But the cemetery—that's a double whammy."

Idiot. I should have remembered. "Her parents died, didn't they? Is that where they're buried?"

"Should have been. There wasn't much left of them to bury." She cocked her head. "She didn't tell you?"

Disappointment hung heavy in my heart. Why had she kept this from me? "No."

Carmen placed the carton of ice cream into the basket over her arm and then opened the freezer to grab another. She shoved the second into my hands. "You're going to need this."

I didn't have a freezer in my hotel room, but I accepted it anyway. "I need to know what happened to them." For some reason, I suddenly needed to understand Sophie more than anything else in the world.

"I agree, but it isn't my place to explain."

"Carmen," I said impatiently. "I'm leaving on Monday, and then it will be too late. Please. I'd like to understand."

"Why?" she asked, suddenly defensive. "So you can make her fall for you and then leave forever?"

That stopped me. Why did talking to Sophie feel so important right now when the future of my career was at stake? Why *this* woman with a dozen others in the rearview mirror—short flings that meant nothing? Why her?

Because she was a steak dinner after a lifetime of canned tuna fish. Because I felt more alive with her than anyone else I'd ever spent time with. Because I liked who I was with her around.

"Because she understands me when nobody else does," I confessed. "I'd like to understand her, too, for however long it lasts."

Carmen examined me for a long time before nodding. I felt as if I'd passed some sort of test. "Fine. Then I'll send it to you."

"Send what?"

"You'll see." She asked for my number, and I gave it to her. She scrolled through the camera roll on her phone and tapped away. Seconds later, my phone buzzed.

"This is just for you," she said pointedly. "Nobody else.

You can't even tell Sophie you saw this, and you're going to delete it right afterward. Swear it."

"I promise. Thank you. Will you bring her some flowers too?" She needed to know that I saw her pain, even if I didn't completely understand it yet. That she wasn't alone in this. I paused. "Actually, I'd rather bring her some myself."

"That's more like it." Carmen winked and headed for the front of the store. My fingers felt frozen, and I realized I'd been holding a carton of ice cream for several minutes now. I slid it back onto the shelf and walked out without buying anything. I couldn't remember what I'd come for in the first place, but whatever it was, I had something far better.

I slid into my seat and opened Carmen's text to see a video. I hit play before even closing the car door.

There sat Sophie on a stool, her white button-down shirt fitted enough to suggest her curves without showing them. She fidgeted with her sleeves, which were obviously too long, and avoided looking at the camera. In the background, Carmen's voice said, "Ready?"

"I guess," Sophie said. Her hair was shorter, I noticed. This could have been a few months ago or a couple of years ago. Hard to tell.

Carmen counted down from three, then went silent as Sophie smiled tightly at the camera. "Hello and good morning. I'm Sophie Goodman, and I'm applying for the wildlife technician position. You asked me to tell you my story from the heart, so here it is." She took a deep breath.

I found myself rooting for her inside. She looked so nervous.

"I grew up an only child," she began. "My parents were both born and raised in New York City. They chose to get married in Four Seasons Park downtown, where they'd initially met at a party. Apparently the wedding was a huge event and a bunch of famous people came because my dad was an actor. Anyway, they lived in a tiny apartment for the first two years and had a baby boy. My mom couldn't find a day care she felt was safe, so she asked a neighbor who worked as a nanny. She returned home one day to find her baby dead in his crib and the nanny passed out on the couch. The woman had been doing drugs, and while she was high, she injected him to keep him quiet and happy. He died of an overdose."

She took in a long, deep breath and slowly blew it out. I detected the slightest shudder in her voice as she continued. "My mom was pregnant with me at the time. My parents decided the big city wasn't a safe place to raise a family anymore, so they moved to the small town of Huckleberry Creek, Montana. I grew up knowing nothing different. I spent hours exploring the woods and talking to the birds. Moose, elk, bears—all the animals people fear? I talked to them just like the deer and the squirrels and everything else that lived around me. I just felt like one of them."

She fell silent for a long moment.

"You've got this," Carmen whispered in the background. It was then I noticed the tears filling Sophie's eyes.

She wiped them back with her too-long sleeves and belted a laugh. "Sorry. You said you wanted it from the heart. Anyway, my parents would never let us go anywhere. At first I assumed it was because of money, but soon I realized they were scared. Leaving Huckleberry Creek even for a vacation felt like leaving our haven. As long as we stayed here, our little family would be safe. They felt that way until I was seventeen, when my mom persuaded my dad to return to Manhattan for their anniversary trip. It was the middle of my junior year, and they didn't want to jeopardize my quest for a college scholarship, so my grandma flew out to stay with me and they hired a pilot with a small plane to take them to New York City. They never made it."

My heart constricted. *There wasn't much left of them to bury*, Carmen had said. No wonder Sophie didn't like the cemetery.

"Grammy Marissa made plans to move here, and the town of Huckleberry Creek rallied around us. They became my new family. I also grew to love the wilderness that cradled them even more. I got an online degree in environmental management so I could respect my parents' wishes for me to live here, where they'd felt safe, and work in the forest I loved. But it isn't what I thought it would be, and I—I think it might be time to leave and . . . and . . ."

She fell silent again.

"But what?" Carmen hissed.

Sophie wiped her eyes again and sniffed. "I can't do this."

"Yes, you can."

"Fine. I *won't* do this." She looked directly at the camera. "I'm not ready. I'm sorry." Then she stood and left.

In the background, Carmen sighed and the video ended.

I watched it twice more, understanding sinking deeper each time. It all made sense now—why Sophie loved her town and felt she had to defend it. Why she'd been so adamant about honoring the legacy of the dead. I felt a deep ache in my heart for her and the pain she'd carried alone all this time. So much loss. I wondered that she could smile at all.

The only thing I didn't understand was her odd reaction to my meeting her young friend Nate, but hopefully that trust would come in time.

Time. The one thing I didn't have.

I glanced at the grocery store, which had gone dark while I sat there absorbed in Sophie's interview video. There would be no buying her flowers tonight. I had a better idea anyway.

My thumb hovered over the delete button. Deleting it would be the right thing to do, but her story was so detailed and so *precisely* what I needed for my show. And what if I wanted to watch it again later because I'd forgotten some of the details? My memory was pretty terrible these days.

It sounded like an excuse. Sophie would want me to delete this.

I brought my thumb down again—and pulled it back. What if Sophie miraculously agreed to let me use it? If I saved it instead, Carmen wouldn't have to resend it. And if not, I could always delete it later. There had to be someone else in Huckleberry Creek with a similarly tragic and emotional story. This would serve as inspiration until then.

My mind made up, I sent the video to my files instead and resolved to worry about the show tomorrow. My subscribers could wait.

I had a heart to win.

THIRTEEN

Sophie

As the background music swelled, the hero on the screen swept the heroine into his arms and kissed her deeply. Carmen sighed. I dipped my spoon into the ice cream carton to find it empty and my fingers sticky. Had I really eaten the entire thing in one hour?

"Can't we just end it here?" Carmen asked, clutching her bowl to her chest and frowning at the TV. "I don't like when it gets complicated and something pulls them apart."

"But then when they do end up together, it's more satisfying," I said.

"I know, I know. I just wish they didn't have to suffer so much first." She blew a kiss at the screen. "You were meant to be together, all right? Trust me. I don't know why I'm the one who always has to push people toward their other halves."

I looked at her, amused. "Since when are you the self-designated town matchmaker?"

Carmen looked sheepish. "I, uh, need more ice cream." She stood and swiped the empty carton from my hands before going into the kitchen for more.

A sudden knock on the door had her running back in. "I knew it!"

My heart skipped a beat. "You didn't."

"He was at the grocery store with his puppy-dog eyes, asking about you," she whined. "What was I supposed to do?"

"I don't know—say goodbye and goodnight like a normal person?" I said, hurrying to toss my spoon into the sink. I wore baggy gray sweatpants and a white hoodie with a green paint splatter on the front and only a sports bra underneath. Nothing could be done about that. But I swept a hand through my scraggly hair and scrubbed my cheeks with my palms, hoping I didn't look as exhausted as I felt.

"I can tell him you went to bed," Carmen said, tiptoeing toward the door uncertainly. "It's after eleven."

"Too late." I pointed to the open blinds. He could've been watching me pig out on ice cream for the past ten minutes for all I knew. "I'll get it."

I slid back the bolt and swung open the door to find Tanner standing there gripping a handful of wilting plants dotted with pink flowers.

"Hey, there," he said, shoving them toward me. "I don't know what your favorite flower is, but I figured it wasn't something grown in a greenhouse. So I picked these for you in a field . . . in the dark."

"Aww," Carmen said from behind me. When I whirled around, ready to hiss at her, she shrugged an apology and bolted for her room.

"Thanks," I said, accepting them while examining the buds closely. "I've always wanted a vase full of spotted knapweed."

He chuckled. "Those aren't flowers, are they?"

"Not in the least, city boy." I couldn't hold back a smile now. "I'll put them in water anyway. Want to come inside?"

He glanced at the corner where Carmen now hid, her eyes

barely visible in the dark hallway. "Actually, would you like to go for a drive? There's something I want to talk to you about."

My heart flipped again. Whatever the topic of conversation was, he didn't look too serious. More like apologetic. "If you don't mind that I'm wearing my painting outfit."

He grinned and held out his arm, which I took. "A classic. I left mine at the hotel, unfortunately."

"I'm happy to help create a new one."

"I'm sure you are. Maybe I'll take you up on that sometime." He closed the door behind me, and we headed for his car. "It's pretty late, so I thought we could drive around your neighborhood and talk."

"Huckleberry Creek's Hillside Park Homes," I said in my best announcer voice. "The ultimate travel destination."

He opened the door and held it for me as I slid inside—swoon—and soon we were off. His leather seat contoured to my body perfectly and the interior smelled like oiled leather and mint gum. I kept my hands folded against my chest while he drove. To his credit, he didn't seem bothered by it.

"I know about your parents," he finally said.

"Carmen?" I guessed wryly.

"Sort of, yeah. Don't be upset with her. I wouldn't let her go until I had answers."

"Answers as to why I acted the way I did." Looking back on our earlier conversation, I could understand his bewilderment. I'd been so overwhelmed with emotion, I couldn't deal with the firehose of feelings that washed over me simply from being in his presence. It had all been too much.

He looked at me, the passing streetlight illuminating half his face. "I was an idiot to be so insensitive about the cemetery. It should have occurred to me that would be a difficult place for you."

"It wasn't your fault. Truly." And I meant it. "It's just the timing of all this. Tuesday is the tenth anniversary of the day Sheriff Woodhouse showed up at my door to tell me my parents wouldn't be returning. It's been a hard memory to shake these past few days."

"I'm amazed you've handled it as well as you have considering the circumstances. I can't imagine how painful that was. My parents are both still alive, though they've been divorced since I was three and I barely see either one. I would have been devastated to lose them both at the same time, especially as a teenager."

"My grandma moved in with me, but, yeah. It was hard. Staying here in the same house, walking by their room for those first few months? And then there was graduation and not seeing them in the audience . . . so hard. They were nowhere and everywhere at the same time—the backs of strangers' heads on the bus, the whispers in the movie theater, the echoes of memories wherever I looked. I came home from school once after I got a part in the school play and called for my mom so I could tell her. She didn't answer. It took me half a minute to remember she never would." I took a shuddering breath. What was it about Tanner that brought out all my secrets? I hadn't even told this to Carmen.

"So you feel like you can't leave now," Tanner said. "Because your being here was what your parents wanted."

His voicing my thoughts so accurately, and being the first person I knew who truly saw what I kept hidden in the deepest recesses of my soul, left me speechless for a moment. I fought for control and won, managing to keep the tears at bay and the pain hidden away once again, deep inside where it belonged.

"I know it sounds silly," I said, too lightly. "Grammy moved back to Florida to help her arthritis, but I wouldn't go—not when it meant leaving my safe haven and my family."

"And then that jerkface of a date insulted them at the restaurant, which led me to you," he said, his voice soft.

I met his gaze. The cocky travel show host was completely gone. All that remained was a man whose eyes were open, honest, and vulnerable. A man who *saw* me. Not the person I wanted the world to see, but the real me. Even better, he was showing me who he really was too. He'd taken the first step toward me and waited now, watching to see if I would take a step toward him. Not pushy but hoping. Waiting. Not at all the man I thought I'd met that first night.

I'd been wrong about him. Tanner Carmichael was as far from Alan as a man could possibly get.

"As interesting as my neighborhood is," I said, "there's something I want to show you."

FOURTEEN

TANNER

She directed us toward the national park. I was grateful I'd charged my car this afternoon. By her somber expression, this would be no casual drive. When we reached the entrance booth and the gate blocking the road, she slid out and unlocked it, swinging it open so I could pass. Then she secured it again, plopped into her seat, and slammed the door closed. "Follow this road for three miles and make a right at the fork."

I followed her directions for nearly fifteen minutes, climbing upward all the while. She opened the window and pulled the hairband from her ponytail, letting her hair fly behind her in the crisp fall air. The wind held a deeper chill than at the harvest carnival earlier, but she didn't seem affected by it.

Finally, she told me to park at the side of the road. When we got out, she took my hand. "This way."

The air smelled of pine, crisp autumn wind, and Sophie's citrus shampoo. Her hair still fell over her shoulders in messy waves she didn't seem to care a whit about. Where did this girl come from?

"It's a little bit of a hike," she said, approaching a hill. She whipped out her cell phone and turned on the light. I did the same, and we made our way up a hill and over a series of boulders. I felt a little winded when we reached a clearing at the top. Then I turned to see what she was looking at and felt winded in a different way.

Wow.

A diamond-filled lake spread below us, a nearly perfect replica of the starry sky above. The world was quiet, like a painting, exquisite and beautiful, the only sound the buzz of a mosquito near my ear.

She watched me, expressionless, as if this moment mattered more than all the rest. I wasn't sure what she wanted me to say. I couldn't speak if I wanted to. This moment, this *place*, was the perfect complement to the company.

"I have no words," I finally told her. It was incredible. Life-changing. Somehow, deep inside, I knew something in my soul had shifted forever.

It was the right answer. She nodded in approval, then squeezed my hand before breaking contact to sit on a fallen tree log. "I know. It's hard to talk when words break the stillness of it all, you know?"

"That," I said, sitting next to her, "and the fact that I can't think of a single word to describe this." I took her hand again. She didn't pull away. "Thank you for showing me. I can tell it means a lot to you."

"I've only brought one other person up here, and my relationship with him was a disaster. I'm not sure why I wanted you to see it. It just felt right." She looked away now, but her hand gripped mine more tightly than ever. She said nothing more about this mystery man, and despite my rising jealousy, I knew better than to ask for details.

"I'm honored you would trust me with this," I said.

Now she looked at me, her eyes flashing even in the moonlight. "Are you going to tell everyone now?"

It felt like another test, but I barely hesitated this time. "Not a chance. It's yours, and that's how it should stay." Somehow, the more I learned about Sophie and her fierce independence, the more I wanted to protect her. Even if it meant protecting her from myself.

Her mouth curved into a shy grin, and her eyes darted away, giving me the perfect opportunity to examine her in the darkness. Her hair fell in front of her face in loose, messy waves she didn't bother to push out of the way. It hid most of her, but I'd already memorized the way her jaw sloped into a perfect, long, kissable throat. I wanted to comb my fingers through her hair and sweep it behind her neck so I could taste her lips. And maybe her neck too.

You're leaving soon, an annoying inner voice said, sounding a lot like Carmen. And an even deeper inner voice nudged that I still hadn't told her about Olivia. But I wasn't the same guy who'd proposed to the famous soccer player and tried desperately to keep our relationship together despite her indifference. Not anymore. Not when I was with Sophie.

I cleared my throat, which felt surprisingly raspy. "Uh, so I've been thinking. I have an important question about Huckleberry Creek."

There was disappointment in her expression. "Oh?"

"Certainly. And I can't leave until it's answered."

Her eyes flicked to my mouth. "Well, we can't have that."

"Of course not. Not when you've been counting the days until I leave you in peace."

She smiled with one eyebrow raised. "No, I mean I won't be answering questions that allow you to leave."

That smile—it was a mischievous, dangerous, adorable thing, and it captured me like a fish on a hook. My hand lifted slowly to her face, brushing the hair from her cheek. She leaned into my touch, so I cradled the back of her head and brought her face ever so slowly to mine. My lips hovered just above hers, asking. Wanting. Waiting, ever so impatiently.

She closed her eyes. I felt her breath on my lips, considering.

Then she slid her arms up my chest and around my shoulders and pulled me to her, practically crashing her lips onto mine. There was nothing coy about this kiss. She'd made her decision, and she was 1,000 percent in.

I deepened it with an involuntary growl, which made her grin against my mouth. Something about Sophie captured me, and I couldn't even pinpoint when it started. This girl didn't just have my body like the others—she had my heart, and deep inside, it terrified me how easily she'd stolen it right from my chest.

We spent about a century like that until I found her on my lap, her fingers tangled in my hair and her face soft against the rough stubble of my chin. Our breaths came in hard gasps and I longed for more. Far more.

Even as the thought came, I pulled away and rested her head against my chest, breathing hard. That was the old Tanner, the one chasing a life that followed in his father's footsteps. The man I'd been before Olivia came along and broke my heart, leaving it shattered in a hundred pieces. The man I had to resist becoming again.

Sophie was different. If I meant to win her, I had to be different too.

"Again," I breathed. "I have no words."

"Then stop talking." She pressed her lips against my jawline, soft and warm, and I shuddered with desire.

No. Not tonight. Not now, when she'd been crying earlier.

"I think we should get going," I told her, every inch of my

body wanting exactly the opposite. "You have church in the morning, and I . . ." I had hundreds of clips to edit, most of which held secret glimpses of Sophie. But they would be nothing like this moment, here and now. "As much as I would like otherwise, we should take this slow. Do things right."

She pulled back and looked at me. *Really* looked. "You mean that, don't you?"

"I'm trying to." My voice still sounded like a sick frog, so I cleared it again.

She smiled and stood, letting her fingers trail along my arms as she did. "You're not who I thought you'd be, Tanner Carmichael. This version of you is irresistible." She waited until the last second to break contact, and then there was just the cold air between us, the distance feeling like a hundred miles.

"Is it too late to change my mind?" I croaked.

She laughed—a glorious, happy sound I could have listened to forever. She took my hands and hoisted me onto my feet. "Come on. We still have two more days."

The sobering reminder felt like tying an anvil to a cloud. Even as she said it, her smile faded a bit.

I swept the hair out of her face once more, grinning to see that it had gotten far messier in the past hour, or however long we'd been here. I cupped her face in my hands, lightly brushing her cheek with my thumb. She gave a cute little sigh, and her eyes fluttered slightly.

"If I promise not to leave town until I absolutely must," I said softly, "will you answer the question I've been dying to know?"

"Now you're dying?" She leaned in for a quick peck. "I had no idea you were so dramatic."

"It's a YouTuber thing. My question is this." I paused. "If

you could go anywhere in the world, all expenses paid, where would you go?"

She blinked. "That isn't about Huckleberry Creek."

"Indeed it is. It's about Huckleberry Creek's most important part."

Her smile grew soft. "Four Seasons Park."

Now it was my turn to be surprised. "Where your parents were married?"

She looked at me strangely. "How did you know that?"

Uh-oh. I'd promised not to tell Sophie about the video. "Carmen . . . told me."

She chuckled wryly and slid into my embrace. "Of course she did. Well, ever since my parents passed, I've felt like something was missing. I just want to know if I'll find it there by finishing what they began." She looked up at me and cocked her head, but she couldn't hide the shine of unshed tears in her eyes. "That probably doesn't make sense."

"It makes perfect sense. You have a beautiful soul, you know that?"

She snorted and wiped her eyes, looking around as if awakening from a dream. "Now don't go accusing me of things like that. Are you ready to leave?"

Her question suddenly held double meaning. My schedule was a tight one. In three days, I was due to arrive in Columbus, Ohio, then a city in Michigan after that. I didn't have a single day to spare. Yet I found that for the first time in years, I had absolutely no desire to leave. I wanted to stay—not for an extra day or even a week but forever.

It terrified me.

"No," I said. "But we can go anyway."

FIFTEEN

Sophie

KISSING TANNER CARMICHAEL felt like leaping off the rocks at the falls—my stomach dropping beneath me as I sailed through the air, knowing the ground would find me any second but enjoying the descent anyway.

Despite kissing the man I'd sworn to drive off, the world still turned. Carmen still went to work the next morning and left her usual blender mess in the kitchen. I went to church alone and listened while the organ played before the service, trying to sort through way too many thoughts. I even touched my lips once, remembering what his mouth felt like against mine, wondering if it was all real or some kind of cruel dream.

So when my phone buzzed with a new text, I opened it in record time.

I had fun last night, Tanner had texted. *Thanks for helping me experience the best part of Huckleberry Creek.*

I grinned. My overlook was the most scenic spot in a hundred miles, but I had a feeling he wasn't talking about that. What did a YouTube star with a trail of smitten fans see in a forest ranger from Montana?

I grinned and typed a response. *I had fun, too, even though you tried to poison me with weeds first.*

His reply came quickly. *I was testing your forest knowledge. You passed. I also have some good news for you.*

Which is? I wrote.

Seconds later, his reply came in. *You won the Most Beautiful Woman at Church Award. Congratulations.*

I looked around. There sat Tanner a few rows back. He winked. If he'd been handsome last night with his black tee and windswept hair, he was utterly stunning in his gray suit—a different one from the wedding, surprisingly—with his hair slicked back. He looked like a movie star. By the reactions of those around us, I wasn't the only one who'd noticed. Lucille entered the room in a bright-pink dress that barely covered her rear end, and made a beeline for his pew.

The version of Tanner I'd watched on the YouTube channel would have urged her to sit by him. He would have flirted with her, used her in all the ways she wanted to be used, then said goodbye at the end of his visit without a second thought. The entire congregation watched him now, seeming to expect just that.

But the real Tanner nodded politely to her, excused himself, and stood to make his way over to me. Then he took a seat at my side and put his arm around my bare shoulders. I could practically feel Lucille's furious glare burning through my back. Whispers peppered the audience.

If Huckleberry Creek didn't know we were dating before, they certainly did now. The realization made me surprisingly giddy.

Tanner leaned over. "The prize for your award is in my car. Don't let me forget to give it to you afterward."

"If my reward is a make-out session in your Tesla, I have a nice bouquet of wildflowers to give you." Not that it didn't sound like heaven. Simply thinking about a repeat of last night, his fingers tangled in my hair and his lips on my neck, made my cheeks burn.

He didn't seem to notice. "Actually, it's something I bought for you," he whispered. "Although with your town's active gossip network, you may already know what it is." He nodded his head at the women across the aisle, who openly stared at me as they whispered to each other. They seemed pretty interested in this gift, which meant it was a good one. Or, heaven forbid, something risqué. My entire face felt hot now. Did I look radioactive, or did I just feel that way?

Tanner saw my expression and chuckled. "I just realized how that sounded. That's not at all what I—oh, man. It's a Conservation Club sticker. I gave a donation to the forest preservation fund and got a sticker. That's *all*." Now his face flushed as well.

I felt the laughter bubble up and placed a hand on my mouth to keep it inside. Soon we both giggled like children, our shoulders bouncing, tears springing to my eyes. The pastor reached the podium and shot me a stern glare.

Less than a minute into the sermon, I suppressed a new wave of laughter over today's topic: *loving our enemies*.

Three days ago, Tanner had been my enemy. I wanted him gone and would do anything it took to drive him away. Now I wanted him to stay and would do almost anything to keep him here. What changed?

Not him, I realized. *Me.* My heart changed. Maybe not changed as much as opened just a bit to give him a peek inside. Surprisingly, he hadn't run away at what he found there or hacked it to pieces like I'd expected. Maybe the ground wouldn't meet me in this free fall as quickly as I assumed.

I spent the next forty minutes floating in Tanner's minty scent, acutely aware of his arm around my shoulders and his thumb stroking the top of my hand as he held it. Every inch of my body that ran against his felt as if on fire. I also felt the entire congregation's eyes boring into the back of my skull. Before long, the service ended and people began to file out the door. I heard mine and Tanner's names whispered more than once.

He didn't seem to have noticed when he stood, intertwining his fingers with mine to avoid breaking contact as I rose to my feet. It sent a series of delighted shivers through me, which I convinced myself was the air conditioning. Finally, the chapel emptied except for the pastor, who hurried toward the door with a sharp, upturned eyebrow in my direction and nothing more. He hadn't approved of my dating Alan, either. I chose to believe it wasn't a sign.

As we followed Pastor Grey toward the exit, walking side by side, I wondered what this particular walk would be like in reverse—with me wearing a white dress.

Then I reminded myself I wasn't marrying Tanner Carmichael. I wouldn't even be dating him after tomorrow.

The thought made my floating sensation dim somewhat as we entered the sunshine outside. The church ladies had already set out food for the luncheon, my homemade rolls—Mom's recipe—among the spread. A few of them smiled at me knowingly. Others . . . didn't, looking in every direction but mine while wearing frowns. Because, apparently, shameless flirting at the carnival was okay for those married church ladies but holding his hand as a single woman wasn't. Tanner saw someone struggling to set up a chair and immediately left my side to help.

After the blessing on the food, we waited in line for a few minutes and piled food onto our plates. Tanner let me go first and kept one hand on my lower back while carrying his plate with the other. When I handed him a roll and told him I'd made them this morning, he swiped one, sank his teeth into it, and groaned. "You have my heart, Sophie Goodman."

"You know what they say about men and hearts," I said, grinning back at him.

"Better be careful. Now that I know you can cook, I may have to extend my trip a day or two. This may sound very 1960s of me, but I've never had a woman cook for me before."

"Besides your mom?"

He snorted. "Only if you count mac 'n' cheese. She didn't like cooking, so we always ordered out. Same with Oli—" He snapped his mouth shut.

I paused in the act of reaching for a cup, frozen in discomfort at his expression. "Who?"

"Never mind. Let me get that for you." His hand left my back, and he poured me a cup of chilled cider, his face suddenly closed off. Then we headed toward a couple of empty chairs at the nearest table. "You know, there's something I still need for this episode that I haven't found yet, and I'm beginning to worry."

"What's that?"

"An interview. A solid, personal story that pulls at the heartstrings."

Was he hinting at mine? Because it wasn't for sale. I felt my hackles go up and tried to smooth my expression as I sat and put my plate on the table. "You could try Doc Susan over there. She might have some interesting stories."

"I talked to her at the reception. Interesting, but not what I'm looking for."

"Why don't you interview Mari, the baker? Or those farmers from the other day? I'm sure they have some pretty funny stories."

"Sophie." He gave a self-deprecating laugh and shook his head. "I'm asking if you'd consider letting me share yours."

I stared at him, letting his words sink in. Then I continued in a rush. "How about Helen, with the black hair and bright-red dress? She has seven children. Some of her stories are hilarious. Oh, look—she's coming over here."

"Sophie." He put his hand over mine as if to quiet me. "At least consider it. I know a lot of people would be touched by what you've been through. But if you aren't comfortable with that, all you have to do is say no."

"No."

His hand recoiled for a second, his eyebrows raised in surprise.

I forced a smile. "Sorry. You're right. I don't feel comfortable with that. Thanks for asking first. I don't mind being in a few clips, but I don't want them to know anything about me."

He studied me for a long moment, disappointment in his eyes, and finally nodded. "Okay. You have my word."

Just then, Helen arrived with a plate of food in one hand and a toddler in the other. "Are these seats taken?"

"They're all yours. Helen, have you met Tanner?"

"No, I haven't," she said, grinning so wide I could see every single one of her straight, white teeth. She'd worked as a dental hygienist once upon a time. "Nice to meet you, Mr. Carmichael. My kids are obsessed with your show."

She found a seat and started to ask questions between bites and directing her little ones. I watched Tanner carefully, but he seemed to have gotten over his disappointment already. None of our earlier tension remained. Every smile, every laugh, every question was genuine, and he seemed to be truly interested in what Helen had to say. He even pulled out his phone and asked her to repeat something so he could record it. Maybe it would all be okay after all.

After the luncheon, we helped clean up and carry the tables to the storage shed behind the chapel. Mari, wearing her bakery name tag even though everyone knew her, grabbed my elbow when Tanner wasn't looking and pulled me over to whisper. "I hoped you would snag him before he left town. You've always been a smart girl."

"I don't know if he's officially snagged," I replied, watching him single-handedly carry a table like it was nothing. His sleeves did little to hide the muscles flexed beneath, and I wasn't the only one noticing. Lucille stood in the corner with her arms folded, pouting, her short dress seemingly unnoticed by her target.

"Oh, he's snagged. I've been watching how he stares at you." Mari gave me a quick side hug. "Your mama would have liked him, too, I bet. Much better than that Alan character. This is one you can trust with your heart."

I swallowed at that, hoping she was right. "But how do you know? He's only been here five days."

"Sometimes five *minutes* is long enough to know. Your heart will tell you if you listen to it. In fact, I remember your mama giving me similar advice before I married Calvin. It took me months to accept that she was right, and I'd been guided all along."

I stared at her. "You never told me that. You two are such a perfect couple. What stopped you from jumping in?"

"A previous heartbreak. Trusted someone I shouldn't have and then stopped trusting my feelings when the right one came along. Deep down, I think I felt I deserved to be punished. That I had to atone for the first one before I could truly be whole for the second. You know?" She peered at me as if looking into my soul. "No, you probably don't."

I took a deep breath and released it, feeling the internal conflict ease a bit. "You'd be surprised."

She clapped her hands on my shoulders. "Well, then. Trust me when I say you deserve this. Lord knows you've suffered enough. Happiness will find you if you don't drive it away before it can take hold."

"Thank you, Mari," I said, squeezing her hand. "I don't know where I'd be without you."

"The whole town would be slightly lighter without me, I wager," she said, patting her soft tummy with a laugh. "Oh, but pastries do soothe the soul. Come by sometime so your boyfriend can try a few."

That meant bringing him by in the next thirty hours because Tanner intended to leave tomorrow by sunset. But I didn't want to dampen her smile, so I nodded. "You bet."

Feeling rooted to the floor with the weight of the moment, I watched her carry the empty pastry boxes away.

Deep down, I felt that I deserved to be punished, Mari had said. *That I had to atone for the first one before I could truly be whole for the second.*

Did I feel the same way about Alan? Had I been scared of my instant chemistry with Tanner and concocted a reason to hate him because at my core I believed I didn't deserve to love again?

Near the parking lot, I caught sight of Nate in his wheelchair. He watched a group of kids playing ball with a wistfulness that stabbed my gut. He seemed happy most of the time, but like most kids who'd survived terrible accidents, he seemed to have moments where reality hit harder than others.

"Everything okay?" Tanner asked, wiping his dusty hands on his pants and coming to a stop in front of me. "You look a little sad."

For the first time, I realized he wasn't wearing his camera. "Did you leave your equipment in the car?"

"It's in the trunk. I'll grab it if I need to. Today is about us." He cocked his head. "How can I help?"

My earlier worries melted away at his open expression. No

walls, no secrets. There was only one way to know for sure whether Mari was right about him. I glanced at Nate again. "You haven't asked about featuring Nate's story."

Tanner followed my gaze and brought his own immediately back. "You said he was off-limits. It never even crossed my mind."

I examined this man who seemed to know my every thought before even I was aware of it. Tanner had been respectful last night and sweet today and pretty much the opposite of Alan in every way. He was far from the player he portrayed on YouTube. I could see it now, the man he truly was, and my heart swelled with happiness.

I'd let him into nearly aspect of my life, and he'd thrived there, but there was still one very important element missing.

"I don't want you to feature him," I said, grabbing Tanner's hand and pulling him toward Nate. "But I do want you to know him."

His surprise turned into realization, then understanding. "Are you certain?"

"I am." We stopped in front of Nate and I winked at the boy. "Hey, buddy. Look who I found wandering around again. Should I send him away?"

Nate's giant grin filled my entire soul. "Not a chance. Hi, Tanner. Am I going to be in your show?"

"Probably not, sport. But if I need a partner, you'll be the first to know. Well, maybe the second." Tanner took my hand again and gazed into my eyes until my legs felt like the raspberry gelatin just served at the luncheon. "Sophie will always be my first choice."

Nate groaned. "You guys are gross."

"Sorry," I said, tearing my eyes back to Nate. "I need to talk to Tanner for a bit, but do you need anything first?"

"No." His attention had already returned to the game, his eyes following the ball.

"See ya, sport," Tanner called as we walked away. Then he looked at me curiously, still gripping my hand. "I feel like that was an important moment, and I don't know why."

"I'm about to tell you. But this conversation needs to happen in the right place." I led him around the corner to my favorite street—the one currently lined with blazing-red maple trees. The slight breeze rustled the leaves on the quiet road, leaving us feeling like we were completely alone in the world, at the edge of a brilliant flame.

His reaction was worth it. "I didn't know that color existed," he said reverently. "Such a bright red. Now I regret leaving my camera behind."

"If you had your camera, I couldn't tell you my story," I said. "Except it isn't all my story. It's partly Nate's."

"I'm listening."

I led him to the bench swinging from one of the trees in the Parkers' front yard, knowing they wouldn't mind. The couple was out of town most of the year anyway and had told me to use the bench anytime.

I took a deep breath. "It all started with Alan."

So I told him. I explained how a man had come to town and swept me off my feet, making me believe I loved him. Making me believe he wanted to stay forever and start a family with me. The entire town expected a proposal any day. But deep down, something nagged at me. I couldn't quite pinpoint what it was. And then I'd seen the text.

"I managed to sneak a peek at his phone one day," I said, "and discovered my suspicions were backward. I thought he was cheating on me, but it was worse than that. He was married and *I* was the mistress he was cheating with."

Tanner growled something under his breath.

"I confronted him, and we broke up. I remember how angry he was—I thought he would hit me. But he stormed off and went to the bar even though it was barely four in the afternoon. The next thing I knew, there were sirens downtown. A lot of them." My voice wavered, so I paused to gain control. "I followed the sound to find a barricade and a crowd. There, I saw Alan's crumpled car, and . . . and the ambulance."

"He hit Nate," Tanner breathed.

I nodded, staring at my hands. They swam in my blurry vision.

"Oh, Sophie." He swept a wayward hair from my face and lifted my chin upward so I had to face him. "No. This was not your fault. You have to know that."

"I know," I managed. "At least, my brain knows. Alan made his own choices, and I would never choose this. But my heart doesn't quite believe it. I'm reminded of that day every time I look at Nate. If I'd confronted Alan sooner, Nate would still be walking. Or if I'd waited to confront him until the next day, even."

"Then he could have hurt someone else. Killed them, maybe. Whatever would have happened, it was on him, not you. Never you." He stroked my cheek, leaving a trail of heat behind. "So that's why you feel so protective of this town. Because you believe you failed them once."

I tore my gaze away, fixing it squarely on the flame trees. This time, my voice was firm. "I can't let anything hurt them—or me—again."

He fell silent.

"I'm not saying this is over," I said quickly. "We both knew it would end when you drove away. I guess I'm saying I was wrong about you and I trust you with Nate. I trust you with Huckleberry Creek. And I trust you with my heart, for however long this lasts."

He took my hand again and placed it between both of his. "It doesn't have to end tomorrow."

My head jerked up. What was he saying?

"I was going to ask you tonight. Now, don't answer right away. I just want you to consider it and let me know later." He took a deep breath and plunged in. "I'd like you to come with me."

I didn't know what I'd expected, but it wasn't this. I thought he'd ask for a long-distance relationship. But traveling together? "You mean to the next town?"

"And the one after that, as long as this lasts. And I think it could last a long time." He squeezed my hand, the warmth of his palms sending a shock wave of alertness up my arm. "Sophie, I felt reborn when I met you. There's something incredible about you that I've never experienced before. I knew your town would be special, but I didn't realize it could produce a woman so confident, so carefree and different. Whatever this is between us, it isn't something I'm willing to leave behind." He lifted my hand to his lips and kissed it. "Please come."

My brain felt like mush. "I—I have to think—"

Then his hand was brushing my hair aside again, his fingers tracing my face, his lips on my jaw. I turned my head so our lips met. Suddenly his kiss took on a whole new level of ferocity. My insides seemed to blaze far brighter and hotter than any autumn tree on a quiet small-town street.

Leaving meant saying goodbye to everything I knew and loved. I'd only known Tanner for a few days. This was all happening so fast.

I reluctantly broke the kiss. "Can I have a few hours to decide?"

"Of course. As long as you plan to spend those hours with me." He wrapped his arms around me and pulled me even closer, his lips finding mine again. I allowed myself to get lost in his embrace, his kiss, his minty scent, everything. I could sit here like this forever while the world turned around us. Mari said happiness would find me if I let it. If this wasn't pure and undefiled happiness, I didn't know what was.

"Interesting place for a make-out session," an unfamiliar woman's voice said.

Tanner went rigid and slowly pulled away, leaning back so I could see the woman standing on the sidewalk before us. She had red hair that almost matched the trees, a brown cap, and skinny jeans tucked into tall boots. But what chilled my heart was the smirk she wore. "Figured I'd find you wooing some poor fool, Tanner."

"Olivia," he choked, looking positively dumbfounded.

SIXTEEN

TANNER

"What—why are you here?" I stammered. "H-how did you—"

"Find you?" Olivia broke in. "I just followed your trail of broken hearts." She looked Sophie up and down with a frown. "Took quite awhile. You've been busy."

I rose to my feet, standing protectively in front of Sophie. "You have my number, Olivia. If you needed something, you could have called."

"You wouldn't have picked up the phone anyway."

She was right. I wouldn't have. Even now I wanted to walk away, but I knew she'd just hunt me down at the hotel. This bulldog sunk her teeth into whatever she wanted until it yielded to her will.

I spoke through a clenched jaw. "Tell me what you want and leave me be."

"Only a teensy little favor. Remember those videos of us together in the beginning? Turns out those were good for my career. When we broke up, ticket sales for my team took a nosedive. Now they're threatening to trade me to the Sassy Lions."

She sniffed. "Can you imagine, living in rural Iowa, of all places? Anyway, if you feature me again, we can fix all that. Two, maybe three episodes should do the trick. And if something blossoms between us again . . ." She shrugged.

I shook my head in wonder. She'd probably timed her interruption for the most inconvenient moment possible. Behind me, I could feel Sophie's walls going up. "You are something else, you know that?"

"Of course. That's why you proposed in the first place. Or did you tell your girlfriend about that?"

"Olivia," I said, ignoring the sharp gaze boring into the back of my head. "We broke up two years ago. If you insist on stalking me, I'll get a restraining order."

My ex smirked again. "Don't get your manhood in a tizzy. I'm only asking you to include me in your show for a while. I was helpful before, and I can be helpful again."

I knew her better than that. It couldn't possibly be that easy. "Or what?"

"Or I'll tell your little hobby here who you really are. She obviously doesn't know, or she wouldn't have thrown herself at you like that."

Sophie leaped to her feet, fists clenched. She sent me a seething glare. "You were engaged? You didn't think that would be important for me to know?"

I opened my mouth to explain, but my brain refused to cooperate. "I was waiting for the right time."

"And the right time was after I agreed to go with you." Her beautiful eyes flashed. "Or after we'd already left?"

I wasn't sure what to say to that. She was right. I hadn't intended to tell her for a long time, and I wasn't sure what that meant. "I didn't want to ruin this."

"And you wouldn't have. Not by telling the truth." Sophie folded her arms. "But a lie would definitely do it."

"I have never once lied to you."

My words had been sincere and soft-spoken. It was that fact, perhaps, that made her lower her voice. "Maybe not intentionally. But there are all kinds of lies. Tell me this. If I look you up online, will I find more about what your friend here is talking about?"

We both knew the answer to that question. So did Olivia, by the victorious smirk she now wore. My name was linked with years of celebrity gossip adding up to several hours of reading material. Jill and I had done our job well—the world wanted Tanner Carmichael to be a player, so we'd given them what they wanted. Frankly, it wasn't all that different from the truth.

I'd presented Sophie with a different version of myself—the Tanner I wanted to become. The Tanner she deserved. But she didn't deserve this.

"That's what I thought." Sophie shot an ice-cold glare at Olivia before leveling it on me. "Have a nice trip." Then she stalked away.

"Sophie!" I called, a note of desperation in my tone. "I'll come over soon to explain. Just let me take care of this."

"I have no interest in hearing any more lies from you."

"But—"

She whirled to face me. "I'm going to pick up Grammy from the airport. Don't drive over to visit me, and don't call me ever again." Then she marched off.

"Ooh," Olivia purred. "Maybe she knows more about you than I thought."

I watched Sophie disappear around the corner, feeling a part of me leave with her. This couldn't be happening. "Olivia, I let you find your happiness. Don't you dare encroach on mine."

"You think that's happiness?" she asked, waving in Sophie's

direction. "You can't have known her longer than a few days, just like all the others. I counted at least six since we dated."

I turned to face her, my voice low and cold. "Dated? We were *engaged*. I asked you to be my wife, and you said yes. That isn't something you throw away over a soccer career, especially one so terrible you'd hunt me down and destroy my life to help revive it. How dare you."

To her credit, she actually looked stung. "Tanner—"

"No." It was a word I'd never told her before for fear she would leave. Now that I wanted her gone, it came easily. Then again, I was a different man now, and I'd experienced what a relationship could be—and it wasn't this. It wasn't anything I'd ever experienced before.

"Are you serious?"

"If you'd asked nicely, I might have put you in one of the clips. But when you try to manipulate me into helping you, the answer will always be no."

She pursed her lips. "We had something special once. Surely that's worth one little TV appearance."

She was still stubborn as ever. But this time, I wouldn't back down. Never again. "If what we had was special, you wouldn't have thrown it away so easily."

Olivia sighed and dropped her little act. "You're such an idiot sometimes. I didn't end it because it wasn't real. I ended it because you wanted me to be something I wasn't."

I turned to face her. "What?" She hadn't said this before.

"You wanted someone who would make you dinner and greet you at the door with the kids when you walked in from work. Someone who wanted to live in the same house her entire life and serve in the PTA at the kids' school. I couldn't be that woman no matter how hard I tried." She touched my arm, stroking her finger along my bicep. "And I did try. Did you know I baked you a cake for your birthday once?"

I shook my head, surprise rendering me speechless.

"It came out hard as a rock and tasted like cardboard. I threw it away before you came over and pretended the burning smell came from the neighbors' next door."

"I think I remember that," I said softly. Then I remembered that Sophie was likely sobbing on the drive home, and I snapped back to the moment, yanking my arm away. "And then you chose your career over me, just like always."

Olivia rolled her eyes. "Oh, come on. Like you didn't do the same thing. You were obsessed with your channel, so laser-focused on your own success that you couldn't see anyone else." She saw my flinch and her voice softened. "Look, I didn't come here to argue. Just one little five-minute clip and I'll be gone."

My hackles raised over her accusations. If there was one thing I had plenty of practice with, it was arguing with Olivia. In a moment, I saw exactly how the conversation would go—and it would end up right back here, with me telling her no and her pushing until she got what she wanted.

"It's over," I told her firmly. "You made your choice. Now, leave me in peace to pursue mine." I turned and began to jog away. If I hurried, maybe I could catch Sophie before she reached her house.

Olivia's voice rose just before I turned the corner. "You leave only pain behind wherever you go, Tanner Carmichael. Be glad I helped her see that before she fell too hard."

The old Tanner would have been destroyed by those words. He would have run away, moped for a day or two, and then called her to say he changed his mind and would help her after all. But the old Tanner no longer existed, and something told me I would never see my ex again.

So I halted in my tracks and turned back to face the woman I'd once loved. "I hope you find what you're looking for, Olivia. I truly wish you the best." Strangely, I meant the words.

Then I left her there, gaping in shock.

♥ ♥ ♥ ♥ ♥ ♥

Sophie wouldn't answer the door. Neither would Carmen. I could hear them whispering through an open window, although I couldn't make out the words. I didn't need to. The message was clear enough.

I drove to my hotel room, locked the door, and slid the bolt in case Olivia decided to make another appearance. Then I fell onto my bed and heaved a sigh.

My phone rang. Jill. She was the last person I wanted to talk to right now, but maybe it would take my mind off things. I jammed my finger on the button and shouted into the phone. "What?"

"Whoa there. What's going on with you?"

Olivia was right. I was a grade-A, bona fide jerk. "Sorry. It's been a day, but that's no excuse. What's up?"

"Bet you can guess. I just got a call from Guy's publicist, who told me we have competition. Lacey Style is also schmoozing him. Word on the street is they went to lunch today."

Not good. Not good at all.

I groaned and resisted the temptation to send my phone through the glass doors and onto the street below. "We need to get this thing posted right now."

"Like, yesterday. You close?"

"I have footage, raw material, and an incomplete outline." *And a girlfriend who didn't last twenty-four hours.*

"And the big story?"

"Nothing. Just a few little ones."

Her voice held an edge of panic. "Guy won't get five seconds in without a good hook, Tanner. He was very specific about what he wants."

"Well, turns out I can't find one. A few smaller ones all braided together will have to do. Maybe he'll really like the dinosaur. They have one they move around and dress up—it's pretty funny."

Jill didn't seem amused. "You should be finishing up editing by now, not scraping the barrel for silly clips of plastic reptiles. What have you been doing all this time? What could possibly be more important than this deal?"

I fell silent.

"A woman," she guessed. When I didn't deny it, she sighed. "We're screwed."

When it came to the collaboration, I had to agree with her. If only Sophie had agreed to share her story. It was exactly what Guy wanted—a heartwarming tale of growth and courage with a beautiful subject who connected deeply with people. My subscribers would fall for her as quickly as I had.

Olivia was wrong. Maybe I had been obsessed with my channel before, but somehow, Sophie had managed to fill that hunger in my heart. All I could think about was fixing what lay broken between us. An eight-minute episode could never matter as much as that.

"You know what?" I said slowly. "This is your moment. I'll send you everything I have, so see what you can do with it. I'm sure you can put together something dramatic and emotional."

"You trust me to put it all together, start to finish? The episode that could make or break our careers?"

"Sure. You have a better sense for entertainment than most in this industry."

"True, but—"

"Have it in my inbox by midnight and I'll give you half the

ad revenue from this episode and from whatever comes of Guy's collaboration."

"Done."

She'd spoken too quickly, almost as if expecting the offer. This partnership with Guy would make us both millions. *If I could make it happen.* The possibilities that rendered me giddy in the past now felt muted, like they lay behind a thick blanket. Their siren call didn't have quite the same power, not when it required leaving Sophie behind.

Sophie. She wouldn't answer the door or my phone calls, but maybe she'd see a text.

I wished Jill luck and hung up. Then I sent her all the files from my phone and laptop in an uncharacteristic mess before texting Sophie. *Sorry about Olivia. I sent her packing in a big way. I'm pretty sure she won't be bothering us again. By the way, those other women meant nothing.*

Then I read the words, deleted them, and shook my head in disgust. Sophie deserved better than excuses and defensiveness.

I should have told you about Olivia, I wrote instead. *I'm sorry. Please let me explain.*

I waited two minutes, then five, then ten. No answer. She'd probably deleted it immediately.

Leaning back on my bed, I started at the yellow-stained ceiling. This goof-up required far more than a bouquet of flowers . . . or, in my case, a bouquet of forest weeds.

My phone rang again. I answered before noticing who it was and let my shoulders slump when my brother's voice, not Sophie's, came through the speaker.

"You sound so excited to hear from me," Ben said, laughing.

"Sorry." I'd said that word a lot today. "I was waiting to hear from someone."

"A woman." When I didn't refute it, he chuckled again. "You never change, little bro."

I'd heard that a lot today too. "Anyway..."

"So, we invited you over for Thanksgiving, and you haven't answered our calls or texts. Mom's worried. I thought I'd make sure you're still alive and report back to her."

"Still alive last time I checked." Last night, I'd felt more alive than ever. It contrasted sharply with this moment, when dread kept my jaw clenched tight. "I should have answered. I appreciate you and Emily inviting me, but I'm not going to make it."

There was a long silence. "That's it? You're not going to tell us why?"

"Too busy with the show. I don't have a single day to spare."

"Not even for your family?"

I opened my mouth to snap back, but he was right. I'd been avoiding my family for years. Being around my mom and her sighs of disappointment at my choice of lifestyle didn't exactly feel festive.

"Look. I don't know how to say this," Ben said softly. "But Mom isn't doing so well."

That caught my attention. "What does that mean exactly?"

"She's been in the hospital twice since Christmas. She wouldn't let us tell you because she knew you'd worry, but I think she was hoping you'd find out and come running."

I sat there in shock. How could they keep this from me? "Is she okay?"

"For now. Her heart defect has been acting up, but the doctor doesn't want to do surgery because it might kill her at this age."

I sat forward, not caring that I was shouting now. "But she's only in her sixties and healthy otherwise. They need to take care of this."

"That's what I thought, too, but it's complicated. If you come for Thanksgiving, we'll arrange a quick phone visit with the doctor, and you can ask her all your questions."

My world felt upside down, stacked atop my head with no relief in sight. "I can't make any guarantees, but I'll try."

"Good. I'll tell her."

"Ben?"

"Yeah."

I hesitated. "When you were in the navy, was it hard to have a long-distance relationship with Emily? Eleven months is a long time, and you did it twice."

"Yep, the hardest thing I've ever done in my life. But she was worth it." He paused, then a note of interest appeared in his voice. "You seriously thinking about a long-distance relationship?"

"No. Maybe." I groaned. "I don't know."

"Then your relationship isn't going to make it, because you have to know 100 percent she's the one for you. And, no offense, but you don't exactly have a strong record in that department."

I groaned, suddenly weary of being lectured about this. "Let me sum it up and save you the trouble. I'm a self-absorbed lost cause who's obsessed with his work and avoids his family. Did I forget anything?"

My brother paused. "Obsessed, yes. Maybe a little self-centered too. But it's more like your channel has become your identity, and not a healthy one. Like no amount of attention will ever be enough. It's almost as if you've become . . ."

"Dad," I finished for him, and muttered a curse. Not because his accusations were harsh, although they were, but because there could be a grain of truth to them. My work had indeed become my entire life over the past years. I didn't know how to unravel it all and start again without the whole thing coming completely apart. Even if I mended things with Sophie, where did she fit? Life on the road had never been great for my relationship with Olivia.

My brother wisely changed the subject. "Do you like this woman?"

I lay flat on the bed. "She's different, Ben. She's funny and mischievous and smart. So smart. She's completely different from the others and . . . she's everything." I meant every word.

"Then you're going to have to make some sacrifices for her."

"Like what, quitting the channel? You didn't quit the navy for Emily."

"That's not what I meant."

"Then what *did* you mean?"

He sighed. "Tanner, I know Olivia ripped a giant hole in your life. We can all see that. And I know you've been trying to fill it with other shallow relationships, but that's not how it works. You have to lay your heart on the line again sometime."

I wanted to deny it. But, as usual, my brother—who also had excellent legal advice from his lawyer mind—was right. Maybe Olivia, too, as much I hated to admit it.

"I know," I said softly. "The scary thing is, I think I already have."

"Then I wish you luck, little bro. You're going to need it."

When we hung up, I grabbed my keys and did a quick web search on my phone. I had a beyond-brilliant idea for an apology gift. Any other woman would find it strange, but Sophie wasn't any other woman.

Ready or not, I was taking this to the next level.

SEVENTEEN

Sophie

"Let me guess," I heard Grammy say to someone in the entryway. "You're Tanner. Sophie told me all about you this afternoon. What do you have there?" By the sheer volume of her voice, she wanted me to overhear. And by her enthusiasm, she hadn't listened to a word I said today as I wept and babbled on the way home from picking her up from the airport. She'd ended up driving because I was in no condition to—a fact that left me humiliated and Grammy happy to be able to help.

Tanner said something I couldn't make out, his voice sending an odd shiver through me I liked but also resented. What was it about the man that held me rooted in the kitchen, hiding behind the refrigerator and also hoping he'd come find me and sweep me into his arms? His voice set my heart racing and my skin shivering all at once. Clearly, my body was as confused as my heart.

"Sophie!" Grammy sang. "Your man is here, and he looks very sorry. Don't you, young man?"

"Couldn't be sorrier," he called. I could hear the grin in his voice—sheepish and mischievous.

Well, he wasn't going away on his own. I'd have to send him away myself or it wouldn't happen at all. I stepped around the corner and came to a stunned halt, gaping at him. "Is that a tree?"

Tanner stood in the entryway, gripping a huge pot with a baby evergreen bursting from the top. He tried not to look strained, but from the way the veins in his biceps popped through the tanned skin beneath his T-shirt sleeve, it was heavier than he made it look.

"A ponderosa pine, in fact—native to Huckleberry Creek and the northern Montana wilderness as well as your official state tree."

I reached the doorway, barely noticing Grammy sneaking off with a smile. "You did your research. I'm impressed."

"Good. It took me the entire way here to memorize that. Which took four times longer than normal, by the way."

I chuckled despite myself, feeling utterly disarmed and reluctantly charmed. "Why? Did you carry this all the way here by hand? I'm guessing it didn't fit in your car."

"You'll see. Can I, uh, put this thing down somewhere?"

I gestured to the front yard. "I'd tell you to leave it inside, but these are definitely outdoor trees. Besides, it can grow to 180 feet tall, so . . ."

"Good call." He set it down by the front porch and stood back expectantly. I hadn't intended to join him outside, but he seemed excited about something, and my curiosity got the better of me. I stepped off the threshold and burst out laughing. "You're kidding."

"No, ma'am," Tanner drawled, gesturing to a pair of saddled horses, one of which was attached to a cart. "I would have been here sooner, but Bessie here decided to drop a pile in someone's driveway. It was a bit of a challenge getting it cleaned up, but I managed to accomplish the task unarrested and ready to take you for a ride if you'll allow me."

I held back a giggle, giving the palomino a pat. "Bessie? These are Joe Stanton's geldings."

He shushed me and put a gentle hand on the palomino's nose. "Don't judge. He can go by any name he pleases. Right, pal?"

I eyed Tanner and the horses he'd gone to all this trouble to secure, feeling the familiar warmth I'd gotten used to over the past few days. Then I remembered Olivia and her cruel words and even crueler accusations and felt my brain wrestling my heart once again. Did I truly know Tanner? I thought I had, but four days wasn't long at all.

I took a step back and folded my arms. "I told you not to drive over."

"I didn't. I rode." He unhitched the cart and retrieved the reins, which he'd wrapped around a low tree branch. "You were kind enough to tell me your story. Now I'd like to tell you mine."

The conflict raged inside. He'd be leaving tomorrow, and telling him no could mean a clean break. But something deep inside urged me on. An old memory surfaced about my parents arguing. They'd spoken in whispers, taking turns to express their concerns and perspectives. I remembered being surprised at their level-headedness at the time. Surely a few minutes to hear Tanner's side wouldn't hurt. And Mari *had* told me to give him a chance. A real one, which I hadn't done earlier.

"So Joe let you take his horses just like that?" I asked.

"I persuaded him with a hefty deposit. I guarantee he's hoping something goes wrong and I never return these beauties. Don't worry. I fully intend to disappoint him." He lifted the saddle flap, tightened the cinch, tugged down the stirrups, and held out a hand to me. "Need a leg up?"

"You know more about horses than you let on, cowboy." I grabbed the pommel instead of his hand, placed my left foot in the stirrup, and swung astride. The stirrups were still a little long, but that wasn't a big deal.

He laughed and followed my lead, swinging astride "Bessie," who was actually Bear. A pack bulged behind the saddle. It seemed more surprises lay in my future.

"I may have taken lessons as a kid," he admitted. "English style, though, not Western."

I stared at him, suddenly seeing him in a whole new light. "I can't see you in a pair of breeches and a coat, performing dressage."

He shook his head, adjusting the reins in his hand. "I preferred jumping. Wanted to be in the Olympics someday, but turns out it isn't a career for the poor. How about you?"

"It's been a few years," I admitted. "I liked barrel racing."

"Why does that not surprise me?" He grinned. "Well, we may both be a little rusty on a horse, but I decided you've shown me around enough. Now there's somewhere I want to take you. Follow me, little lady."

I laughed, wondering where he could possibly take me that I hadn't already been. Then I recalled the past few days, full of new and exciting moments, and realized that he already had. Olivia excluded, the last week had included some of the best moments of my life. Fitting that we'd create one last memory now, something that I could remember forever. I patted my horse, swallowed hard, and tightened the reins.

We took Harris Trail out of town and up into the foothills, the crisp autumn wind whipping my hair aside and caressing it with the enchanting scent of pine and the Montana wilderness. Then we reached the tree line. I spotted our destination as we drew near. He'd set out a blanket with a bucket of now-melted ice containing a champagne bottle. A few orange leaves had blown across the blanket.

He dismounted and opened the pack. I recognized the contents immediately—sandwiches from Stella's shop. She would have told him my favorite was the turkey bacon club and likely sent along a few extras just for kicks.

I didn't know what to say. This must have taken all afternoon to arrange. "I figured you'd be spending the day with Olivia or editing." I'd managed to keep most of the bitterness from my voice, but not all. Just thinking about that woman and her perfect hair, athletic body, and expensive clothes made me want to puke—preferably all over her pretty boots.

Above all, knowing Tanner once loved her enough to want to marry her, and maybe still did, hurt like a spear through my rib cage.

Tanner dismounted, secured the gelding, and headed around to help me. But he placed a hand on my horse, looking up at me with nothing but earnestness. "I turned the editing over to my assistant. My days here are limited. I can't waste a single second that I could be spending with you. And Olivia—well, that's what I wanted to explain if you'll allow me." He offered a hand. I didn't need it to dismount, but the offer combined with his words made me feel like some Regency lady in a ball gown, so I took his hand and swung down. A rock I hadn't noticed sabotaged my landing, nearly sending me to the ground, but Tanner's arm swung around my waist and kept me upright. Then we both stood there, my arms on his shoulders and his around my waist and the both of us staring at one another.

We were close enough I should have felt his breath on my face, but there was nothing. He seemed as breathless as I felt.

"Sophie," he whispered, still holding me tight as if expecting me to run again. "I'm so sorry about Olivia. Truly.

Sometimes I wonder what I ever saw in that woman. She hurt me once, and it took me a long time to get over it. But what matters more is that she hurt you, and I can never forgive her for that."

"So she doesn't want you back."

He shrugged. "Maybe, maybe not. She's in the past. You are my present—you and only you." He swept a piece of hair from my face and tucked it behind my ear.

I became fully and painfully aware of everywhere our bodies touched—his chest against mine, our stomachs, his hand pressed against my lower back, holding me against him—and my heart pounded like I'd just run a race. My legs even betrayed me by shaking like a lovesick schoolgirl. *Come on, brain. Work.*

I forced myself to look him right in the eyes. "And what about the future?"

Tanner sighed. "Well, you see, I was going to charm you with my wiles and overpriced sandwiches and warm you up to the idea, but since we're on the subject . . . my invitation still stands. But you don't need to answer yet. We have a few things to work out first."

He didn't have to explain what he meant by that. His ex-fiancée was in town, and he'd spent the day ignoring her and trying to win me back—me, who he'd known for five days. Surely that counted for something.

There was just one more problem . . . a gigantic one.

"And what about Olivia's accusations?" I said quietly. "The other women. Saying she knows who you really are and I don't."

He took a step back, but his hands slid down my arms to take my hands so we didn't break contact. "Come on. Let's sit for this."

We made our way to the blanket. He took a seat and patted

the spot next to him. I broke free of his touch—it muddled my brain—and sat as far from him on the blanket as I could, folding my legs and facing him warily.

He noted my posture, a glint of disappointment in his eyes, and plunged on. "I've never talked to anyone about this before. Not even my brother, who knows pieces of it."

I nodded.

"I told you my parents divorced when I was three. What I didn't tell you was that my father had a string of girlfriends when I was younger. Typical story. My mom took the opposite route, refusing to date and rejecting men entirely. She turned all her attention to us and never remarried. We weren't allowed to discuss Dad at all. I think she secretly hoped he would come crawling back, but he never did."

That sounded terrible. "How sad."

He looked down at his hands. "You'd think I would have learned from my dad's mistakes. I did see the pain he caused. But I spent a summer with him once and saw the world through his eyes. He believed that true happiness was always elsewhere, away from home, just out of reach. He found glimpses of it with many women rather than a single person he promised to love forever. Both of my parents seemed miserable, so I wasn't sure who was right. I'll admit that I met lots of women during my travels and found plenty of fleeting glimpses myself, but nothing substantial. So when Olivia came along, I decided my dad's way was wrong and I was ready to commit." He released a long sigh. "I was, but she wasn't. I bought us a house and found a buyer for my channel so I could be with her on the road. That deal was almost final when I surprised her with the house. She just stared at the keys for a minute and called everything off, right then and there."

I stared at him, swallowing back the tightness in my throat. "So you felt that your dad's way could be right after all, that choosing one woman could only lead to heartbreak. And you returned to your old life."

"I tried, but that way of life went stale pretty quick. Those women left me feeling emptier than before. Although I've met plenty since then, I haven't been with a woman in almost a year."

I nodded, resisting the urge to brush my hand along his frown and the thickening stubble that surrounded it. "That's why you left your family behind. You've been traveling ever since, trying to find happiness where your parents failed."

"I've been avoiding going home because I'd have to face the fact that I've become my father." He paused and chuckled to himself. "It's funny, actually. I was thinking about my dad, feeling sorry for myself while sitting in this cheap Italian restaurant one night, when the woman in the next booth picked me up, slapped me in the face, and turned my life upside down—which, ironically, put it right-side up again." He reached out to place his hand over mine.

I didn't pull it away. In fact, despite what he'd just told me, I wanted to take both of his hands. "Interesting. That's not the way I remember it."

"It's exactly what happened."

"If I'm to be accused of slapping you, I'd prefer to actually do it. Because it would have felt really good a few hours ago." My tone was playful, but my smile was real. I could almost see the walls between us crumbling. In my heart, I felt the truth of his words. Tanner Carmichael had opened his soul for me alone, and I really liked what I saw there.

His chuckle turned into an easy laugh. "I can't imagine moving on without you, Sophie. Exploring this town with you has been the best time I've ever had. But I have to admit that getting to know you has been infinitely better. I never knew someone could be a delightful mystery full of unexpected questions to be answered and riddles to solve yet also feel like home."

"I feel like home to you?" I murmured, feeling drunk in his voice. I wanted him to stop talking and start kissing me already.

"The best home in the world. And I would know."

At his words, the memory of Alan's wrecked car and the ambulance reared its head. When I shoved it out of my mind, an image of my parents' headstone replaced it. All my fears seemed to rise up at once, that shrill internal siren screaming that this wasn't safe, wasn't comfortable. This moment felt way bigger than jumping from the top of a waterfall. It felt like climbing onto the biggest airplane in the world with the intention to jump out without a parachute. My shoulders tensed and my heart galloped faster than any palomino.

And it felt glorious. Like a bird who had just discovered her wings and couldn't wait to use them.

"Then we'd better not make you homeless," I said meaningfully.

His eyes widened, and he grasped my shoulders. "Please tell me you're saying what I think you're saying."

I nodded.

He brushed his lips on my nose. "You've made me the happiest man in the universe."

"Excuse me. My lips are down here, sir."

Before I'd even finished speaking, his lips were on mine. His mouth claimed me like a man wanting far more but barely holding himself back, one hand supporting my head and the other pressing me against him from behind.

Then there was nothing but him, only him, ever Tanner and always.

♥♥♥♥♥

When I went to work early the next morning, the patch of aspen trees shading the booth had begun to turn a brilliant yellow in my absence, a striking contrast to the silvery green fir trees lining the road. I'd always believed autumn was nature's last brilliant, fiery flare of life, and today I felt that more than ever. If I'd chosen not to go with Tanner, our relationship would have been in the autumn stage right now, the clinging-to-life-until-it's-gone stage. The he's-leaving-tonight stage.

But I would be going with him. In a few hours, we'd climb into his car and say goodbye to my town for a good while. My steps were light, my thoughts even lighter. The moment I saw Paul, I would give him my notice and not even feel guilty that there wasn't a replacement lined up yet. Then I'd turn my back on him and that booth forever.

I was free. My inner seventeen-year-old would finally have the adventure she craved . . . and experience it with someone who held her heart, utterly and completely.

Paul's truck didn't show during the first hour, which seemed to drag for at least six. The booth was full of empty cups and wadded gum wrappers from my absence, so I tidied everything, glancing at each car that approached—mostly SUVs and trucks and the occasional minivan with a family. Not a red Tesla in sight. Not that Tanner would be coming here. He would pick me up at my house after work. My suitcase was already packed and waiting by the door. A little thrill shot through me at the thought.

By 9:03 a.m., I couldn't wait any longer. I lifted my radio. "Paul, I need to talk with you. Can you stop by the booth?"

The radio went silent for ten seconds before coming to life

again. "Actually, meet me at the lodge in twenty," Paul's voice said through the static. "I'm sending a temp down to take over for you."

The "temp" turned out to be an intern from a community college a few towns away, a tall girl with a huge smile and a good attitude. I showed her how to use the register and gave her my radio, wondering if she would be taking my place. If so, she'd do a fine job. Then I hopped into my truck and drove to the lodge, which was more log-cabin shack than lodge.

To my surprise, a balding man and a trim woman in full business attire sat next to Paul at the meeting table as I entered. They smiled and rose to their feet. They must have been agency management from Missoula.

"Sophie Goodman," the woman said. "We just arrived, and Paul said you were on your way. It's so nice to meet you in person. I admit I'm fangirling a little right now. I'm a longtime Tanner Carmichael fan. Please, have a seat."

I blinked in confusion. Word of our relationship already reached so far? "Nice to meet you too. Is there something I can help you with?"

"As you know, Paul is retiring in just over two weeks, so we're appointing a replacement for him. Kenneth Vawdry initially indicated an interest, but the Forest Agency has long sought to hire management team members who connect well with our millions of visitors each year. After what we saw this morning, you fit that criteria perfectly."

What they saw this morning? "I'm sorry? Were you watching me work?"

The man laughed. "Of course not. She's referring to the video. You've become quite a celebrity over the past few hours."

I stared at them both, then looked questioningly at Paul. His frown only deepened.

Then it hit me. "Tanner's episode. It launched this morning?"

"Indeed, and it's on track to break records," the woman said. "Four hundred thousand views, last I checked. That's a lot of people coming to know and like Sophie Goodman, Forest Agency Management in Huckleberry Creek, Montana. It has a nice ring to it, don't you think?"

I'd been in a few clips, and there was the one of me jumping into the waterfall. But a deep unease settled in my gut, telling me there was more going on than I knew. "I don't have cell service this far into the canyon. Can you pull up the video, Paul?"

"Of course." He seemed all too eager to put on a show of helpfulness for these people. They must be high up indeed. He opened his laptop and turned it around so we could see. "Here it is." The video already filled the screen, which meant he'd seen it too. The man wouldn't even meet my gaze, and his eyes held something I'd never seen before. Guilt?

He tapped play, and Tanner's face immediately appeared, smiling and proud. "This week, I'm in a little Montana town called Huckleberry Creek, and it's everything a small town should be. If you're tired of the grind of the big city and need a place to relax, you need to check this place out. Here are my seven secret things to experience here, plus a special bonus just for you."

Video clips of our time together followed—our day at the lake, the hot pots, and the carnival complete with Benny the Brontosaurus. Even the corpse's barn. As expected, he'd captured me here and there, usually when I thought the filming was finished or smiled at something outside the frame. I hadn't even noticed at the time.

But that was nothing. The very next second, the screen switched to me sitting on a stool, looking uncomfortable and vulnerable in a white blouse and trousers. My wavy hair was shorter and styled in a way I'd hoped looked feminine yet professional.

An unfamiliar female voice spoke now, off-screen. "But it isn't a town's intriguing history or quirks—like plastic, diaper-wearing dinosaurs—that are the heart of its story. It's the people. And one woman in particular captured Tanner's heart on this trip: Sophie Goodman."

The video began.

I had spent *so long* getting ready for this video, practicing and memorizing my words. The wildlife technician position was something I hadn't been ready for, not then and maybe not even now. But this—a glimpse of myself in the safety of my room, daring to dream in a moment of bravery before letting myself retreat into fear again, being flaunted on the internet to hundreds of thousands? My deepest personal and family secrets cracked open for the world to see? It nearly made my stomach turn over.

As that version of me opened her mouth to speak, I saw myself as Tanner would have—a girl exposing the secrets of her soul, precisely the secrets that could bring in ad revenue on a YouTube channel. An opportunity. A story that could be sold.

This was why he wanted me along on this trip. He knew people would connect with this video, this glimpse of courage and vulnerability. They'd want to see more of that. And since Tanner was incapable of being vulnerable on camera himself, I was the perfect partner to further his career. His promise at the luncheon to protect my privacy had been worth nothing at all.

Tanner had been angry at Oliva for trying to use him, then turned around and used me all the same.

I'd been tricked.

The visitors from the city looked at one another. "Uh," the

woman began. "It's apparent you haven't seen it yet. I assume he secured your permission before posting this?"

"No," I said through gritted teeth, struggling to maintain my composure. This was *not* the place to break down. "He didn't. But I know where he got it." Carmen was the only person who could have given it to him. I'd asked her to delete it a long time ago and never followed up to make sure it was done.

It felt like a double betrayal, Tanner and Carmen both. No, way more than that. There had been Mari's advice to give him a chance, the memory of my parents quietly arguing, Grammy's interference . . . practically everyone I knew and loved had pushed us together. Yet the only person who'd been right about Tanner was his ex. She'd tried to warn me and I hadn't listened.

My life was once again a wreck in the middle of an intersection. But this time, it was my heart that had taken the impact and nobody else's. At least I could be grateful for that.

Now Paul looked a little pale. All three of them glanced around in discomfort.

"We can refer you to an attorney," the man offered. "Although I have to say that this can only help you in your career. It's a very touching demonstration of your passion for wildlife and the environment. I doubt you'd get such exposure anywhere else."

"If I wanted exposure, I would have asked for it," I told them and stood. "Thank you for the kind offer. I'd like more time to consider, if you don't mind. I'll be in touch with your office tomorrow." I glanced at the screen, my face now frozen on it in an expression of sadness.

I wasn't sad now. I was furious.

The couple leaped to their feet. "We're so sorry for these unfortunate circumstances," the woman said as the man struggled to repeat something similar. She reached out a hand, and I shook it. "But we certainly hope you'll accept. You'll do a great job running things here."

Not because I had experience but because I was famous. These people wanted to use me too.

I bid them goodbye and escaped out the door, fighting back angry tears.

♥ ♥ ♥ ♥ ♥ ♥

Carmen reached the house at the same time I did. When I emerged from the car, she threw herself into my arms. "He promised he wouldn't show it to anyone," she wailed. "I made him swear, and he did, and . . . I'm so sorry! I didn't know."

"I know you didn't. He fooled us both." My voice felt distant, cold. As hard as my heart. "Is Grammy still here?"

"She went to visit a friend outside of town. I don't think she knows." Carmen wrapped her arm around my head from behind, almost like a headlock, and dragged me to the front door. "I'm with you, Sophie, no matter what. If you want to make a video to expose him, I'll make sure it gets out there. Want to steal his car and drive it into the lake? I'm in the driver's seat. Seriously. Whatever you need."

I closed the door behind us and embraced her again. "Thank you. I don't know what I would do without you."

And I meant it—because I'd just relearned the lesson Alan taught me long ago. Visitors couldn't be trusted, especially handsome ones. They only brought pain and sorrow to me and the people I loved. Safety wouldn't be found in the arms of a man but in my town and its people. Lessons my parents probably knew all along. And above all, a lesson that hurt more than the others combined.

I didn't deserve real love and could only ever be used.

I retreated to my room and closed the door, leaning against it and sinking to the floor.

"I'm sorry," I whispered to the empty room and the ghosts of my dead parents. "I'll never doubt you again."

EIGHTEEN

TANNER

I woke to my phone buzzing on the nightstand and squinted at the time. 10:04. But wait—I hadn't set my alarm. Had I?

After blinking the fuzziness away, I looked at the screen. This time, I saw that I was getting a call. It disappeared and the buzzing stopped. *You have 4 missed calls,* the screen read.

I sat bolt upright, taking my phone with me and accidentally ripping it off the charging cord. The calls were all from Ben.

My heart practically stopped as I slammed my finger on his name to call him. *Please don't let it be Mom. Please don't let it be Mom.*

He answered right away. "Don't worry. Mom's fine."

I released my breath in a whoosh and sat back, hitting my head against the old-fashioned wooden bedpost. I barely felt it. "Emily, then?" My sister-in-law was still early in her pregnancy, but Ben had said there weren't any complications.

"No, she's fine too. Actually, I have two questions. The brother part of me wants to know whether the woman confessing the deepest feelings of her heart is the one you've fallen for—because she's gorgeous and I'm happy for you if that's the case. And the lawyer part of me wants to know whether she gave you permission to use that video. Because it really doesn't seem like something she'd want plastered across YouTube, and if she didn't . . . we're in big trouble."

His words bounced around in my groggy brain. "What are you talking about? I haven't posted a new episode since last week, and there's no talking woman."

"The one you released last night. Were you drunk or something?"

Last night. I'd been with Sophie, but I'd dropped her off around ten and returned the horses shortly afterward. I hadn't received Jill's email yet with the new episode, so I'd dropped into bed the moment I got to my room. I still wore yesterday's shirt. I lifted it to my face, smiling to realize it smelled a little like Sophie.

Wait. Jill had *posted* the new episode?

The full impact of my brother's words hit me like a hammer to the face. "The video. Is it a brunette woman applying for some wildlife preservation job?"

"Yep. It's a good episode, maybe your best so far, probably because it's so different from your usual fare. But you didn't answer my question. Do we have reason to worry?"

Reason to worry. That was the king of all understatements.

"No, no, no, no," I moaned, grabbing my laptop and slamming it open. It took forever to connect to the hotel's terrible Wi-Fi. I went straight to my channel and froze. There it was—a brand-new episode with my smiling face in front of the Huckleberry Creek Harvest Carnival.

"So you sent Jill a video you didn't want her to use?" Ben asked.

"I didn't mean to send that to her!" I snapped. "It was given to me in confidence by Sophie's roommate. I swore I wouldn't share it with anyone. Sophie didn't even know I had it."

"Oooh. That's not good."

"You think?" I exclaimed, skipping forward in the episode to the last couple of minutes. There sat Sophie in her video, looking vulnerable and brave. I was such an idiot. "I should have deleted it right away. I have to take this down."

"It won't do much good," Ben said with a sigh.

"Why?"

"A bunch of other shows have already picked it up. They're calling her Earth Girl, but I don't think it's derogatory. I think your subscribers really like her. You already have two million views, and it's only been up a few hours. Just think what will happen now that most of the U.S. is awake."

Including most of Huckleberry Creek. Sophie was supposed to work today—had she seen it too? I slammed my laptop screen closed, the movement almost dropping the phone tucked between my shoulder and my ear. *Two million views.* Most of my videos didn't reach that for weeks. Of course my audience would make *this* one go viral. "How can you be so calm right now?"

"It'll only be an issue if Sophie decides to press charges. We won't know our next course of action until we know how she feels."

I knew exactly how she would feel. That was the worst part about all this. "I have to talk to her. I'll call you back."

"Good luck, little bro. You're—"

"I know. I'm going to need it."

"Yep."

As I hung up, a knock sounded on my door.

I looked down at my rumpled clothing, which was still mostly intact, and made my way to the door. I slid it open to find Sophie standing there, her eyes pink but mostly flashing with anger. She wore her work uniform and stood with her arms folded across her chest.

"Sophie," I breathed. "I was just going to find you. I have to explain—"

"There's nothing to explain. This is what you do, and I should have seen that from the beginning."

"What I do? But—"

"You use people. You get close to them, take what you want, and then move on to the next. It isn't that hard to see."

I gaped at her. "Sophie, listen to me. I didn't do this."

"Didn't do this?" she exclaimed incredulously. "Then who did, Benny the Brontosaurus?"

"I would never post that without your permission. You have to believe me. It wasn't supposed to be included."

"Enough lies. Take your channel and your red Tesla out of my town and out of my life."

"Sophie. It was an accident to send—"

"No!"

I flinched at the pain in her voice. The woman I'd spent the last sixteen hours shaping my future around stared at me in fury. Then she plunged into the hallway and slammed the door behind her. If there had been a bolt on the other side, she would have used it. Maybe even nailed it shut and set it on fire.

With a blowtorch.

And I would have deserved it.

I sat there, numb, listening to her footsteps pounding down the hall. Away from me, the man who, despite his best efforts, hurt her yet again. Maybe even worse than that Alan guy.

I glanced at the computer screen again, feeling a strange sense of disassociation. My subscriber and view count were shooting through the roof, yet I didn't care about the show right now. I didn't care about any of that.

All that mattered was that the girl on the other side of the door had just stormed away with my heart, and I wasn't sure anything else would matter ever again.

♥ ♥ ♥ ♥ ♥

I should have left right then.

My episode was finished and a huge success. The hotel in Columbus expected me in two days, and it was a thirty-hour drive. I didn't even have much to pack since I lived out of a suitcase. But instead, I watched the episode over and over, falling deeper in love with the girl I'd accidentally betrayed, hoping a brilliant idea would come to me.

A thousand roses and a million trees couldn't repair what I'd done. Even her grandma probably wouldn't open the door if I showed up at her house. Yesterday's picnic had been so innocent, so carefree. I couldn't remember the last time I felt so happy. Not a temporary happiness, either. A full-hearted, deep, 100-percent-in, joyous and seizing-every-moment-as-it-came happiness. My YouTube career was nothing compared to that feeling. It was like uncovering a dream I didn't know I had, achieving it, and then losing it forever.

I couldn't fix this.

After a restless day of texting and calling Sophie with no answer followed by a long, sleepless night, I called Jill. When I explained the situation, she gave an excuse about the competition posting their episode and not being able to get a hold of me, so she'd made an executive decision. It all sounded innocent, but I read the truth behind her words. I had offered Jill half, and those millions were worth the risk of launching the episode without authorization.

She didn't have to say it. The *Tanner Carmichael* show mattered above all else—even Tanner Carmichael.

It felt like holding up a mirror. Jill reminded me of myself, or at least a version of me that I'd never meant to become. A version that saw people as tools to be used and opportunities to be seized. If this was how betrayal felt—being sold out by someone you trusted—I never wanted Sophie to experience it again.

"I promised you half," I told Jill. "And I'll stick to that commitment. But after we hear back from Guy, assuming we ever do, I'm letting you go. I can't work with someone I can't trust."

"Some thanks," she muttered, and hung up.

I packed everything I owned and checked out of the hotel before dumping my suitcase into the backseat of my car. Then I drove to the coffee shop where I'd picked up our drinks the morning of the waterfall excursion. The drive-thru window was still closed for some odd reason, so I groaned and parked.

The moment I stepped inside, I knew this would have to be a quick trip. Half the shop's tables were full, and every pair of eyes turned in my direction. Some looked away immediately; others narrowed into glares.

I sent them a wave and got in line, ducking my head. I'd hurt one of Huckleberry Creek's best, and we all knew it. Of all the days for a store to close its drive-thru.

The cashier's smile froze when it was my turn. She was young, maybe eighteen. Her eyebrows drew downward in a fierce way, and I knew she recognized me. "You're still here."

"Not for long. I'm on my way out." I gave her my order, and she entered it.

"A lot of people will be happy to see the backside of you," the cashier said, taking my payment card. Then she paused. "That came out wrong. I mean, we'll be happy to see you go."

"I don't blame you," I said, accepting the cup a worker behind her handed me. At least the service was fast when a coffee joint wanted you gone. "Take good care of Sophie, okay? She deserves the best."

"At least we agree on that," a voice called from across the room.

I turned to find Sophie's grandma sitting at a table in the corner beneath a wide window with a clear view of Main Street.

"You really mean to slink out of town like a whipped dog, Tanner Carmichael?" she asked with raised brow.

I approached and nodded to the table. "May I?"

"Only if you want a lecture."

I chuckled and took a seat. "I've been lecturing myself for twenty-four hours now, but I can always use another."

"Not about what you did, although that was pretty thoughtless. The worst part about it is that you'd walk away and leave her alone in her suffering."

I gripped my coffee cup so tightly it dented and nearly spilled all over. *Get a grip.* "Even if I'm the cause of her suffering?"

"If she asked you to leave, it's because she thinks she's better off alone. But it isn't true. That girl has been trying to shoulder an incredible weight since her parents died. It isn't often she finds someone she trusts enough to help her carry it."

The guilt dug deeper into my gut. "I want nothing more than to take it from her."

"Then, tell me this. Are you the man she loved yesterday or the man she hates today?"

I stared at my cup, feeling more helpless than ever. "I suppose I'm both."

Grammy Marissa leaned forward. "You said she deserved better. So *be* better. Be the man she thought you were, the man who made her smile to herself when she thought nobody was looking and sing badly in the shower."

I gave her grandma a half smile. "She did those things?"

"That and more. Didn't hear when I talked to her, got all domestic again and started cooking things . . . Seriously, please distract her. I don't think I've washed so many mixing bowls in all my life."

We chuckled together for a long moment.

Then Grammy Marissa sighed. "Do you realize how long I've tried to convince Sophie to move to Florida? Yet she meets you, and six days later she's ready to leave everything. You made her so happy. Just last night, excited and full of joy, she told me about what life on the road with you would be like." She leaned back and draped her arm over the empty chair next to her. "Of course, it was never about the places. Sophie is content with the simple life. She just wanted to be with you. She still does. She just doesn't know it."

Either Grammy Marissa wanted to dig the knife in deeper or she genuinely wanted me to make things right with Sophie. I chose to believe the latter. "But how? She won't talk to me."

"She doesn't have to talk. All she has to do is listen."

"I tried explaining, but she wouldn't have it."

"Then don't give her a choice."

She wanted me to do something, but what? Just then, my phone buzzed. I slid it from my pocket and checked the screen. Ben again.

"Excuse me just a second," I told her, then answered. "Hey, can I call you back? I don't have any answers for you, but I'm working on it."

"It isn't that," Ben said, his voice grave. "Mom's in the hospital again. It's bad."

I nearly dropped the phone. This couldn't be happening.

"Tanner?" he asked. "Are you there?"

"I'm here. Just processing."

"We all are. Might be a good time to come."

"I'll be there as soon as I can."

He thanked me and hung up. A little dazed, I slid my phone into my pocket. When was the last time I'd actually texted my mom? I couldn't remember. Most of my communication with the family came through Ben. She probably thought I was mad at her. While I'd complained about my mom to Sophie, my mother had been living what could possibly be her last days of life.

Mom had her issues, but she'd still been an excellent mother to her two boys. I, on the other hand, had been a rotten son.

"Bad news?" Grammy Marissa asked with a frown.

"It's my mom," I said, rising to my feet and grabbing my coffee. "I'm sorry. I know you have Sophie's best interests at heart, and you're probably right about everything. I should fight for her." I swallowed hard. "But maybe this is a sign, evidence that what we had was too perfect to exist in this world. She was always too good for me, and now she's figured that out."

"Don't you start on me too. Both of you are worthy and deserving of love no matter what has happened in your pasts to make you believe otherwise. Wherever you go from here, Tanner Carmichael, you remember that."

NINETEEN

Sophie

Normally, walking into Mari's bakery meant the smell of hot butter and cinnamon. Today, it meant a room full of people turning in my direction like someone controlled them with a remote. All women, all wearing the same expression of pity. Sounded like word had gotten around that my video was not, in fact, one I wanted shoved in front of twenty million people. At last count, Tanner's subscribers had shot up another ninety thousand in a day and continued to soar. He'd been right about needing a story, and he'd gotten exactly what he wanted.

"I thought how brave it was that you wanted to share your story," the cashier, Barb, said as she handed me a maple bar on a napkin. My favorite. "Then I kept watching and realized it wasn't something you'd ever agree to post, and I just got so mad that Tanner Carmichael duped us all. Curse his pretty face, am I right?"

The other women nodded in agreement.

"He didn't dupe me at first," I said, keeping my voice even despite the emotions too close to the surface. "I suspected he would do something like this. That's why I wanted him out of town."

"And now we all understand why."

Indeed.

"Just make sure you're ready for the influx of entitled tourists," I told them. "They'll be here any day now."

Mari emerged from the back with a fresh batch of chocolate chip cookies. She handed them to the cashier and came around the counter to give me a warm hug, her bright-white apron and tee a stark contrast to her dark skin. "They've already begun to trickle in. The hotel's two-thirds full, and most of the rentals have been filled for the week. But don't worry. You gave us enough notice that everyone's on high alert. We'll show them a good time and then help them on their way." She patted me on the shoulder. "Oh, girl. Why don't you come over to my house for some iced tea after work? I'll distract you from this dreadful day with some sweet rolls."

I never said no to her sweet rolls, but I didn't feel up to it today. "Another time, if that's all right. I have some things to do."

"Let me know when you're free, then. We'll make a party of it. Maybe watch a chick flick and pretend like there's still a Mister Darcy or two out there for us." She winked. My mother's best friend had never married, which was odd because she was the chick-flick queen of the town.

"Sounds good. I actually came to get something for Grammy. She's been needing something to distract her from the arthritis." I pointed to the raspberry rolls. "Three of these would be perfect."

"I bet the warm Florida weather has done her good," Barb said, scooping them into a box for me. When I tried to hand her my debit card, she waved me away as always. "Mari would fire me if I let you pay. Tell Grammy hi for me."

"That's right," Mari said, following me out the door. Then she wrapped her plump arms around me. "How are you really doing?"

"I'm fine."

She examined me with probing eyes. "Maybe so, but how is your heart?"

I gripped the cardboard box more tightly, feeling tears sting my eyes. "Not fine, but it will be."

"What Tanner did was wrong, and I'm sorry. That was a cruel thing to do, using someone like that. But I'm more sorry that it's over. You looked so happy. I haven't seen you smile like that in a long time."

I looked at her in surprise. "I'm happy here. This town is my family."

"And we'll always be here for you. But I've worried for a long time that you've outgrown what we can offer you. That woman on Tanner's video? She reached for her dreams, and I'm proud of her. I don't recall ever hearing anything about it, though. You didn't send it in, did you?"

I shook my head.

"Why not?"

I swallowed back the ache in my throat. That wasn't a question I knew how to answer. When I finally spoke, my voice was quiet. "Did you know Mom was obsessed with bridges before she married Dad?"

Now it was her turn to look surprised. "Bridges? Why, no, I didn't."

"Neither did I. I found a box of photos she took of the bridges in New York. They were good too—shot from angles I didn't even know were possible, all in stunning black-and-white. I saw a new world through her eyes." I clasped the box against my chest, not caring that its contents were getting smashed. "She loved it there once, and I don't even know why."

Mari pressed her lips together. "She never talked about it. I'm sure she had a thousand good memories that balanced out the bad ones, though, or she wouldn't have tried to go back."

"But she was wrong to do that," I said softly. I'd never voiced it, and I felt a little of the weight lift from my chest to say it. "If they'd stayed here and enjoyed what they already had, everything would be fine now. Every source of pain in my life came from out there, Mari. From reaching too high or venturing too far or someone traveling too wide. Trees have it right. They find a good place to plant their roots and choose to find happiness right where they are. That's what I intend to do."

Mari cocked her head. "But, baby girl, trees don't get to love, and that's the biggest shame of all."

In a moment, I felt seventeen again with all the pitying looks and offers of food and Mari's arms around me, none of which could entirely fill the gaping hole in my heart. Ten years had passed as of today, and I still couldn't say my heart had fully healed. I wasn't sure it ever would.

Tanner hadn't caused that. He'd only reminded me that it was there—and that I would never be fully whole as long as I refused to mend it.

"Thank you," I told my mom's friend. *My* friend.

"I'll always be here," Mari said, squeezing my arm before opening the door to her bakery. "No matter where you end up."

I got into my car, set the box on the seat, and tried to decide where to go next. I wanted to head home, put on my pajamas, and sulk in my room—but I knew Carmen and Grammy wouldn't allow it today, inventing reasons to barge in and start a cheerful conversation. So I drove in the direction of the one place in the world I knew I could be alone.

Thirty minutes later, I arrived at the overlook. I sat on the dead log and tried to take in the view that usually healed my soul. I reminded myself how beautiful it was, how much I loved this forest, and told myself it was enough and would always be enough. But every inch of this cliff felt tainted with Tanner now. The place next to me where he sat, my left thigh where he'd rested his hand. The splotches of autumn color across the forest signifying the approach of winter. The remains of the tree I now sat on that had met its demise long ago, a western larch, probably close to a century old.

I stroked the rough bark, examining it in detail. These trees could live up to five hundred years, but this one had been toppled in a violent storm the same year as my parents' funeral. Was that why I felt drawn to this particular spot and not the cemetery when I thought about my parents? Because it made me feel closer to them?

I followed the log with my eyes to its broken stump, then straightened. Something tiny and green had broken through the soil at its base. I stood and walked over, bending down to get a good look. A new western larch coming up from the same patch of soil. A little late in the season for a tender shoot to be growing, but it looked like a stubborn little thing. Maybe it would survive. Maybe in another ten years it would be tall enough to provide shade for my visits.

The thought of sitting right here in another decade on the twentieth anniversary of my parents' deaths plucked at my injured heart. Who would I be then? What would I accomplish before that day came?

I stared at the little shoot struggling to survive and felt a strange kinship to it. It felt like my heart's struggle to love again. Alan had made me retreat into the dark sanctuary of fear for a long time. Tanner had coaxed me out of it, at least for a little while. Surely that meant something, but I couldn't tell what.

I took my seat again and drew in a few deep, long breaths. Then I did something I should have done a long time before. I stopped ordering my heart not to feel and instead started to listen.

And what my heart told me stunned me into silence.

Tanner or no Tanner, I was ready to love again. Trust again.

Dream again.

I didn't want to spend the rest of my life corralling people away from moose and directing bear traffic and sawing apart fallen trees. Anyone could do that. It would be easy enough to try and preserve what the earth already offered, to keep it the same against forces that wanted to tear it apart. But that felt neutral, safe. The same. Beige. Blah. Like Carmen, I wanted to splash some color onto life. I wanted to make the world *better*. Save a species. Make a difference. Like this tree, I wanted to leave something new behind. Educate people. And I wanted to do it while seeing the world.

Maybe Tanner and I weren't so different after all.

I remembered the thrill inside when we'd kissed, how his hand felt against my back and his full, *genuine* smile. Surely it hadn't all been a lie for him. But whether it had been or not, I knew it hadn't been a lie for me, and that was significant.

It felt like a little green shoot inside, ready to grow into a new tree.

And as fragile as it felt right now, I was happy to see it.

TWENTY

TANNER

Jill called as I walked through the hospital, looking for the right room number. Annoyed, I sent it to voicemail. I found the room and opened the heavy hospital door, tapping gently on the wood. Ben sat on a chair next to the bed, bouncing his toddler daughter on his lap. Emily sat at the opposite side, her large shirt not quite hiding the baby bump. All three smiled as I entered and closed the door.

Between them, Mom lay asleep in the bed. She had no less than four monitors around her with IV lines and who knew what else connected to her frail body, thin beneath the sheet. Her bright-blonde hair, which she'd dyed ever since I was a child, held more strands of silver than usual. Her eyes were closed, her chest moving slowly. Her skin had a pale-green tint that made me nervous.

"She's resting," Ben said. He stood to hand his daughter to Emily over the bed, then approached me. "Let's talk outside."

"There's nothing you can say out there that I don't already know," Mom said, her eyes still closed. Her voice was quiet, but the strength behind it eased my worry a bit.

"Heart attack," Ben said, shooting Mom a grim smile. "An 86 percent blockage in her artery. They put a stent in shortly after I called you. They also fixed that faulty valve. Or I guess they didn't fix it but put some kind of ring inside it they're going to keep an eye on. Supposedly the valve defect and the chest pain today are unrelated. I was too relieved to hear she was okay to remember all the science behind it."

I felt my entire body relax. "So she'll be all right."

"About a week to recover at home, maybe two. She'll have to take blood thinners to prevent clots from forming at the stent site, but yes. It sounds like she'll be better off than before."

I slapped my brother on the shoulder. "I'm glad you were here."

"Me too."

He stepped aside so I could approach Mom, who opened her eyes as I drew near. They looked a lighter blue than I remembered.

"Hi, Mom."

"Where's my boy? All I see is a man."

I chuckled. "You saw me over Christmas, remember?"

"Of course I remember. But something's changed since then. I can see it." She reached out, and I took her hand.

Emily and Ben exchanged a look. "We should probably get Kylie to bed," Emily said.

Ben nodded. "Tanner, you okay to stay with her tonight?"

I squeezed Mom's hand. "There's nowhere else I'd rather be."

My phone buzzed in my pocket. I whipped it out to see Jill's name and sent her to voicemail once more as my brother made his way over to Mom, kissed her forehead, and left with his family. After the door closed, I took Ben's chair and leaned over my mother's bed. Her eyes hung heavy, as if even our short conversation had drained her.

"You should be resting," I told her. "Can I do anything for you?"

"Yes. You can stop hovering now that they're gone. They were driving me nuts. I had to feign sleep to get any peace." She returned my hand squeeze and turned her head to look directly at me. "You can also tell me what happened to put such a sad look in your eye. Don't lie to me."

Mom always knew. It was one reason I'd stayed away—she had a habit of prying details of my life from my unwilling lips. But this time, I wanted to tell her everything. For the first time in years, I was ready to have a vulnerable, real conversation. That, I guessed, was the difference she saw now.

"Okay," I agreed, "but I'll make it quick so you can sleep."

"Nonsense. You'll take as long as you need."

So I told her everything that had happened in my personal life since Olivia, all the way up through arriving in Huckleberry Creek. I slowed down then and gave Sophie the time she deserved, including details I didn't realize I'd noticed at the time, such as how her eyes were a doe brown in the center with dark brown along the rings laced with flecks of gold that reminded me of tinsel at Christmas. As the story laid itself out between us, my mother listened intently despite her exhaustion. I almost hesitated to tell her about Olivia's arrival and what followed, but Mom deserved no less than the truth.

When I finished, she sighed. "Well, that settles it. You need to go back to Huckleberry Creek as soon as I'm released tomorrow and get that girl back."

"You sound like her grandmother."

"That's because grandmas are smart. Don't tell me I have to talk you into this."

I scooted my chair closer so I could hold Mom's hand without bending over her bed. "I could use a pep talk, but I think it should wait until tomorrow so you can rest. You just had heart surgery."

"So did you, but in a different way. Yours was more painful, I daresay. Now, hush so I can ask you a very important question. I want to know why your channel means so much to you."

I pursed my lips. "I liked to travel and wanted to meet new people. They say to make a living doing what you love most, so I did. Turns out I'm good at it too."

"I know why you started the channel, but I want to know why you're still doing it. What are your reasons now? Do you still like to travel? Do you still want to meet new people and make a living doing what you love?"

Lifting my leg to rest it on the other, I gave her words the consideration they deserved. After a full minute, I spoke again. "I'm getting tired of traveling. I still like it, but I'd like it better if I had somewhere to land and take a break on occasion."

"It's a start. Go on."

I looked at her thoughtfully. "I do like meeting new people, but they all seem the same after a while. At least, until Sophie. Meeting her was like jumping into a cold pool after sitting in a hot tub too long—a shock but a delightfully refreshing one."

Her lips curved into a soft smile. "And the last question. Do you still want to make a living this way?"

My phone buzzed again. I whipped it out to find a text from Jill. *Big news. Huge. Call me NOW*.

I groaned. "Will you excuse me a moment? I'll be right back."

"This body isn't going anywhere."

I stepped into the hallway and called Jill back, speaking quietly so I wouldn't disturb the other patients. "Hey. I'm at the hospital with my mom. Everything okay?"

"Not just okay. It's great!" There was no indication of her anger from yesterday. Her voice held only excitement. "Guy saw our episode and loved it. He wants to meet with you tomorrow for dinner in New York to discuss a permanent collaboration. It worked!"

"It worked," I repeated numbly.

"I've already notified Ohio that you're rescheduling. I know you're in LA, so I'll arrange for a late dinner to give you enough time to get to JFK. I'll text your travel info over as soon as I can. I'm coming too, by the way. You're firing me, but we still have a deal and I'm not missing this." She paused. "I assume you want to stay with your mom overnight or whatever?"

I'd intended to stay with her longer than that, but now that I knew her condition, I felt better about making this work. "A nonstop flight first thing in the morning would be ideal if you can swing it. Actually, get one for Ben too." I needed my brother there as much as I needed the lawyer in him. He'd be irritated about the timing, of course, but hopefully Emily could hold down the fort for a couple of days in our absence. I'd pay a residence nurse if I had to.

My dream had come true . . . and I barely cared.

I stood there after we hung up, processing the news. The clock was ticking, so I called Ben to explain tomorrow's plan. It went about as well as I expected. The arrangements took longer than I wanted, and when I stepped back into Mom's room twenty-five minutes later, her eyes were closed. I turned down the lights and stacked a couple of pillows on the couch that wasn't really a couch, preparing to settle in for the night.

"It's people who matter, Tanner."

I froze. "You're supposed to be asleep."

Her eyes fluttered open. "If you're leaving tomorrow, then we only have tonight for this conversation, so I'm skipping ahead to the good part. It's people who matter. Not careers, not goals or collaborations or your follower count and statistics."

I went to her side again and brushed her hair out of her eyes. "You overheard."

"Hard not to. You left the door open a crack, and you aren't as quiet as you think you are. Listen—when you spend all that money in your bank account, and your hairline recedes, and your partnership with this famous man is long forgotten, all you'll have left is the people who love you. Every follower in the world can't fill the hole one good partner can." Her eyes crinkled in the corners and she frowned slightly. "Trust me on that."

"Mom," I said softly. "You have us, and you always will."

"Except you won't come back unless I end up in the hospital," she said, unable to hide a smile.

"Then I'm going to fix that. I promise to come back for every major holiday—maybe even weekends in between to surprise you. But will you make me a promise in return?"

"Name it."

I kissed her forehead. "Go to sleep. I'll be right here if you need me, tonight and always."

She closed her eyes and let herself sink into the bed. "You have yourself a deal."

♥ ♥ ♥ ♥ ♥

I'd been sitting here in the restaurant for nearly an hour already, yet I couldn't stop looking around the massive room in amazement. This had to be the fanciest place I'd ever seen—and I'd been to a *lot* of restaurants. The sight before me transcended anything I'd experienced in Paris or London.

Every inch of the restaurant's walls and ceiling was made of glass and much of the floor, which looked down upon a courtyard full of tourists. Even the tables were a delicate glass, which made me set my champagne glass down carefully. My plate was big enough to feed a horse, yet the actual food—marinated steak beneath a fancy pastry covered in sauce—was only a few inches round. Despite its small size, only a few bites left me feeling full. My companions at the table barely touched their food either, my brother included. Ben watched me now and cleared his throat lightly. A reminder to listen. I pulled myself back to the conversation.

". . . already have several high-end sponsors I'll have to convince," Guy was saying. "But I'm fairly confident I can bring them around when they see your numbers from that Huckleberry Creek episode. It's odd, though—I couldn't find it to send them the link on the way here."

"I deleted it," I told him simply.

Everyone at the table—Guy, his marketing manager, his attorney, Jill, and Ben—all looked at me like I'd turned into a Great Dane.

"You . . . deleted it," Guy repeated in disbelief. "An episode that broke the YouTube record for most views in a day."

"There were some legal complications with some of the content," Ben jumped in. "He, uh, did that on my recommendation. He'll be more careful in the future."

"See that you do," Guy's attorney said. She reminded me of my sixth-grade teacher, stern and strict. "There's no such thing as casual mistakes in this business. You could have lost your entire channel."

Everyone nodded in agreement, practically shuddering at the thought as they sat at our fancy glass table.

"But everyone will remember it," Jill piped in. "And he still has all those new subscribers." Her eyes met mine, and I was struck again by the cold focus they held. She only cared about closing this deal because she'd get half. She wouldn't even need another job after this.

Guy dabbed at his lips with a thick white cloth napkin. "It was emotional, to be sure. I have to applaud you, Tanner. I didn't think you had it in you, but the feedback I'm seeing from your subscribers is excellent. I usually don't recommend using such tactics, but it certainly worked for you."

"Tactics?" I repeated. "What do you mean by that?"

Guy laughed. "Oh, you know. We all choose the persona we portray on camera. If one thing doesn't work, we try something else. It requires a deep understanding of what our viewers want and giving it to them. Your supposed story this week was one of the cleverest stunts I've ever seen."

I ignored my brother's warning look. "Every second of that was authentic, just like my other episodes. I don't pull stunts on my channel."

"Of course, of course. That's what I tell people as well." He winked. "There was this one old lady whose dying wish was to appear on my show. If I helped her out, she'd add me to her will and kick off her only son. So I inserted her at the very end, inherited her estate when she croaked, and sold it for half a million. Don't you love this business?"

I gaped at the man. Was he really so calculating?

Was I looking at a future version of myself?

Guy raised his glass. "To our new, 'authentic' partnership."

Everyone lifted their glasses. "To the partnership," they said in near unison.

I flexed my fingers, lifting them toward my glass. Then I balled my hands into fists.

"Tanner?" Guy asked.

I stood, forcing my expensive chair to give way with a squeak. "No."

Jill froze, gritting her teeth. "No to what exactly?"

"No to our *authentic* partnership. No to all of you. No to everything." I dropped my napkin on top of the $500 bite of steak. "This isn't what I want."

"Tanner," Ben said. "There's no going back from this. Are you sure?"

"I've never been more sure in my life." I gave Guy a salute and tossed a stack of hundreds onto the table to cover my team's meals. "Thanks for coming all this way, but the deal's off."

"You can't be serious," Jill said.

"I've never been more serious. Come on, Ben." I turned my back on the table and started walking away.

"That's it?" Guy said. "No explanation whatsoever?"

I turned to face him. "I shouldn't have to explain that subscribers and money aren't the most important thing in the world. Integrity matters more. *People* matter more. I lost sight of that once, and I won't do it again."

"Then you'll fall into obscurity," Guy snapped.

"Maybe. But I'll fall being who I am. Goodnight, everyone." I strode for the door, looking over my shoulder at the table.

Jill watched me leave with a fury in her eyes I'd never seen before. She huffed a moment, smoothed her expression, and leaned over to whisper something to Guy. To my amusement, he waved her off without a glance.

She scowled, stood, and stomped away, heading for the curved stairwell to the lower level rather than following us. Just before she disappeared from sight, she sent a seething glare my direction. It seemed she wouldn't be getting her millions after all.

Ben hurried past me and reached out to hold the door. We passed through to the elevator, where we stood alone as the doors shut. Then my brother stood there, staring at me with wide eyes. "I can't believe you did that."

"I don't need a lecture about rudeness right now. Sorry about dragging you all the way here for nothing, though."

"No, I mean the choice you just made. Tanner, this is huge. I'm so proud of you right now." The smile on his face couldn't be wider. Ben looked at me with the same pride I'd seen in my mom at the hospital last night. Before I knew what was happening, he pulled me in for a hug.

I stiffened. Our family had never been super close, and we rarely hugged. But I slowly put my arms around him too. "Thank you."

"I'd better step it up now, or you'll become the favorite son." He pulled away and chuckled. "Actually, since Emily and I have produced the first and soon-to-be-second grandchildren, I may be safe for a while yet."

"You're probably right about that."

He cocked his head. "Speaking of grandchildren—any word from Sophie?"

I swallowed. Nothing at all. It seemed she truly had moved on.

"I see," Ben said. "What are you going to do? Does she know you deleted that episode?"

"No idea. I didn't delete it for her, though. I did it because using that video was wrong and I'm not that kind of guy."

"You're right about that." He paused. "Although this was a big oops, so it may require a bigger apology than deleting your mistake."

"I've already given her a tree. I don't think I dare give her anything bigger than that."

"A tree?" He looked confused. "Dude. I meant a *big* apology. You don't have millions of subscribers for nothing."

We reached the ground floor, and the doors opened with a ding. As they did, an idea struck me. A perfect, wonderful, glorious idea.

"You're right." I threw an arm around my brother, who tensed as I had a moment ago. "So right. And brilliant and an excellent big brother. Not sure if I've mentioned that before."

He sighed. "What do you want this time?"

I stepped out of the elevator and faced him. "Can Emily spare you a few more hours? I'm going to need your researching skills."

He raised an eyebrow, but grinned when he saw the look on my face. "Count me in. I wouldn't miss this for the world."

TWENTY-ONE

Sophie

Two days after Tanner's video hit YouTube, I quit my job.

Paul frowned when I gave him the official letter to pass along to the Forest Agency. "Is this some feminist crap about keeping you in the booth?" he hissed. "If it is, I don't understand it. You have a real opportunity here."

I did my best not to roll my eyes. If he weren't retiring, I would have told him off then and there. "It's the perfect opportunity for someone else. Thanks for hiring me and helping me find out what I want." *And don't want.* I refused to be used again, by Paul or his bosses or anyone else.

"Where do you intend to go from here, then? I'm sure that wildlife technician job was filled long ago."

I smiled politely at him. "Actually, I've been thinking about a career educating the public in wildlife preservation using social media, YouTube specifically. Those videos can be very effective." I grinned and walked away, leaving him sputtering.

When I arrived home, a little sweaty and more than a little dirty, Carmen burst out of the kitchen with a giant bowl of popcorn that made the entire living room smell like melted butter. "There you are. I thought you got eaten by a bear."

"This *is* the time of year when bears are fattening up for hibernation," I told her. "But they're mostly harmless as long as—"

"Okay, well, anyway," she broke in, rolling her eyes. "I thought we could have a movie night."

I raised an eyebrow. "I thought you had plans tonight."

Carmen looked positively giddy. "Canceled. There's something you have to see." She motioned to the couch. "Sit."

It was then I saw her arrangement of pillows across the sofa and a second huge bowl of popcorn. "How long is this movie exactly?"

"Not long. I'm setting the mood. Will you sit already?"

I sat. She shoved the new bowl into my hands and plopped down next to me. Then she picked up the remote and woke up the TV, which came to life. Tanner's YouTube episode list.

I groaned. "Not a fan already, Carmen."

"Give it a chance. I think you'll like this one." She pulled up one of the videos and hit play before sitting back with a grin.

The sight of Tanner standing there with a tight black V-neck tee that pulled nicely around his shoulders and hardened chest made my heart skip a beat. It was the same shirt he'd worn to the carnival with his ridiculous Grease jacket. And those arms . . . they'd been around me just days before. Those lips had been on mine, and possibly my neck too, and—dang. I would need a fan to get through this.

Somewhere deep down, my heart quivered in its safe little corner. I wasn't sure I could handle another surprise from him. I almost dumped the popcorn over Carmen's head and went to my room.

But this wasn't a past video. The post date said today despite the skyrocketing view numbers. Behind him lay a wide patch of lawn and people walking past on a sidewalk. One couple had a dog and looked at one another shyly, as if this were the exciting new beginning of a promising relationship.

"Today I'm at a park in Manhattan," Tanner began. "Normally, I would tell you all about it, maybe interview the caretaker and show you what's cool about it. But this episode is for a very special person and her alone. The rest of you can hang on for the ride."

I looked at Carmen questioningly, but she shushed me and motioned back to the TV.

"I messed up," Tanner said. "Big time. Not only did I visit a small town with the intention of profiting off it, not caring what happened to it afterward, but I did something far worse. I used someone I cared about. I shared a story that wasn't mine to share. It was an accident, but I should have made sure it didn't happen in the first place. I betrayed her trust in the biggest way possible, and that's on me. Nobody else." The camera moved in on his face—that jaw I'd caressed and those eyes that seemed to stare into my soul, and I saw only truth there. "So I took down my previous episode and recorded this one instead. I can't undo what happened, but I want to try and make it right."

I set the popcorn bowl on the floor and swallowed back the lump in my throat.

"This is Four Seasons Park," he said. "This special person's parents were married here, and she's always wanted to visit. But since I can't bring her here, I'm bringing it to her."

Tears sprang to my eyes. Now I recognized it. That lawn, that pathway behind it, the skyline in the distance. I'd seen it in their wedding photos.

"I did some research. Turns out a local newspaper covered the event in detail back then. Where I'm standing now is where the happy couple stood when they made their vows. Out there," he said, gesturing to the lawn, "is where the guests sat.

And this was the aisle." He motioned to a stone pathway with grass growing between the cracks.

Suddenly, I could picture it—my mother in her white dress with a train that ran at least fifteen feet. My father in his black tux, watching her with a tender expression. He cried over everything. Always had. He didn't like watching movies where people died or fell in love because he got weepy and then grumpy that he'd gotten weepy.

And now it was me acting all weepy. Carmen wordlessly handed me a box of tissues she'd obviously prepared in advance. I grabbed a handful.

The camera moved close to Tanner's face again. "In an interview, your mother said they also met here. That's why they chose this spot for the wedding rather than a church. It was autumn just like now, and she thought the crisp air and colorful trees would make for a beautiful beginning. But the most remarkable part of all this, and probably the reason the newspaper thought the event would be significant enough to cover, was the guest list." He named off a list of famous actors, most of whom I'd heard of. I couldn't believe my father had not only interacted with them in his acting career but known them well enough to invite them to his wedding.

Carmen released a long sob and yanked me closer. "This is just so beautiful."

The screen cut out, and suddenly Tanner was in front of the lake. "Not only did they meet here in the park, but your father proposed right here on the lakeshore. Or rather, he had a friend dress up as the Loch Ness monster and rise out of the water, holding up a sign. I'm told by a witness that it was rather epic." He grinned. "There should definitely be more giant, fake lizards in cities today."

I snorted, not missing the joke about Huckleberry Creek's dinosaur mascot.

The screen changed again, this time to a hotel lobby. "This is the Diamond Atlantic Hotel, just outside the park. It has some of the best views in the entire city. They spent their three-day honeymoon here." The camera framed his face now. "I want to close with a message to this special person. I know you're trying to forget me, but the past few days have been agony. I'm asking you to forgive me. I don't deserve it, but I need it. I need you. I never thought I'd find a place to call home, and I especially didn't think I'd find it in a person. You made me fall for you in a way I didn't think would be possible again."

His lines thus far were obviously practiced and well-spoken, but this time his voice sounded husky, vulnerable.

"Sophie," he said. "I think I just might love you."

Carmen paused the episode on the last screen, freezing Tanner's hopeful, sorrowful, beautiful face. "Okay, maybe the popcorn was a bit much. But it was better than physically tying you to the sofa."

I stared at the TV, an odd mess of emotions running through me. *I think I might just love you.*

"Now what?" Carmen asked, watching the emotions play out on my face.

"He loves me," I repeated in wonder.

"Yeah," she said, her tone rising in a question. "That was obvious in the first minute of the video. So what are you going to do about it?"

A dozen emotions filled my body to the point that it took a minute to sort through them. Carmen waited, quietly watching me as I tried to listen to what my heart said. It wasn't until I calmed the fear writhing within that I could finally hear its gentle whisper. Then I agreed with it, completely and absolutely.

I felt my smile widen. "Carmen, I'm going to need your help."

She straightened. "Absolutely. I'm down. Toilet papering, egging, silent treatment, whatever. Except I might draw the line at murder after an apology like his."

"You can hold on to those for now. We don't have much time to pack."

"Pack?"

"Yes, pack. And call your assistant manager to cash in on those unused vacation days you keep hounding me about. We're going on a road trip." I grinned and dumped my popcorn bowl over her head, making her yelp. "You can pick the popcorn out of your hair on the way."

My best friend leaped to her feet and squealed, pumping her fists in the air and ignoring the kernels hanging from her hair.

Right before dumping her bowl over *my* head.

TWENTY-TWO

TANNER

I stayed a couple of extra days in Manhattan, hoping by some miracle I would hear from Sophie. After another sleepless night, I checked my phone again—nothing—and left the hotel early to find breakfast. The big city had its charms. I liked the constant sound of traffic, the tapping of high heels on the wide sidewalks full of pedestrians, and the smell of cigarette smoke mingling with that of fresh-baked goods. But three days in New York City was plenty. Sophie had converted me to small towns in a big way, and I wasn't sure anything else would ever be enough again.

Ready or not, it was time to move on.

For years to come, I would mourn my stupidity in losing Sophie. I knew that now. But at least I wouldn't spend the next decade chasing a dream no longer important to me. The moment I finished in Ohio, I planned to take an extended break somewhere. Rethink my career. Decide what I wanted my YouTube channel to be since I knew now what I didn't want. *Thank you, Guy.*

I returned to the hotel lobby a few minutes later with a coffee in hand and headed straight

for the stairs—only to catch a glimpse of a woman with a single dark braid standing nearby. She caught my gaze, winked, and walked away. It made me stop in my tracks and stare.

Carmen?

It couldn't be. The chances of Sophie's roommate being in New York and in this hotel, no less, were extremely slim. Microscopic.

Yet I found myself turning to follow. I sprinted down the steps and caught sight of her disappearing around the corner toward the hotel's conference rooms. Odd. There was no conference here today, and she wouldn't be attending one if there were. Sophie told me her friend worked at some small boutique shop, not the large international companies this hotel catered to.

I turned another corner only to peer down an empty hallway. Not a single soul to be seen.

It had to be the two glasses of expensive champagne I'd consumed last night. A deep exhaustion beckoned me to my room and bed and the TV, to a life that made sense and didn't throw mirages of my ex-girlfriends' roommates into the mix.

The woman peered around the corner, caught my eye, and smirked. Then she disappeared again.

No question this time. It was definitely Carmen.

She clearly wanted me to follow, so I did. She darted past several closed doors and plunged through an open doorway into darkness. I paused to listen but heard nothing. Why did I suddenly feel like a child walking into a haunted circus?

"Come in, you dolt," she hissed from the darkness.

I obeyed. The instant I did, the room flooded with light. The small conference room didn't have any chairs or tables set up, but someone had obviously spent hours decorating it. A line of cafe lights hung from the ceiling. Pictures of exotic lands covered three of the walls, and a huge wall-sized map of the world covered the fourth. I instantly recognized the tiny red markings on it as the places I'd featured on my channel.

Sophie stepped out in front of me. "Hello, Tanner."

I gaped. She wore a stunning pale-pink dress that perfectly hugged her curves and a side bun that accentuated her slender neck. Above all, she wore a smile. The combination made my heart soar.

"You once told me I felt like home," she said. "I thought you were sweet-talking me. But when you left, I realized I knew exactly what you meant because I felt homesick. The town I thought was my safe haven, my protection? It wasn't those things anymore. Huckleberry Creek was only a stand-in, a placeholder until I discovered my real home—which, as I found out, is where you are."

"Sophie," I began, that single word encompassing a world of emotion.

"Shh. Don't interrupt, or I'll forget what I memorized. So anyway," she said, formally, and I realized Carmen filmed this from the doorway. "You've seen a lot of the world alone, but there's a whole lot of empty space on that map we need to fill. Together." Her gaze darted to the camera, then back at me. "I think what I'm saying is that I might just love you too, Tanner Carmichael."

I stood there, admiring how her perfect hair fell in soft waves around her perfect face and emphasized her perfect neck. I had every inch of them memorized and suspected I always would—including the shy smile she now wore.

"So?" she asked. "Are you going to say something? Actually, I should clarify. We have some new cities to see, but only the ones we can drive to. I'm not sure I'm ready to fly yet. Oh! Or maybe we can take a cruise ship—"

I swept her into my arms and silenced her with a decisive kiss.

She returned it hungrily, and I deepened it, forgetting we were being filmed until Carmen cleared her throat. "I think . . . um, yeah. Definitely going to turn this thing off now."

Sophie pulled away and chuckled. "Sorry."

"For the record," I told them, winking at the camera, "I'm not sorry. Not a single, tiny bit."

And I kissed her again.

TWENTY-THREE

Sophie

"It's so nice to chat with you," Grammy's warm voice said through my phone's speaker. "Are you sure you have to go? All my neighbors are out of town, and bingo night got canceled, so we can talk all night if you want."

"There's someone I need to see," I whispered. "Someone who seems a little lonely and maybe needs a friend."

"Aw, that sounds nice. Such a good girl. But why are you whispering?"

I grinned at Tanner, who quietly counted. "One. Two. Three."

We jumped out of the bushes at the side of Grammy's house and yelled, "Surprise!"

Grammy, who was sitting in a white plastic chair in her tiny backyard, dropped the phone into the grass and squealed, whirling around in surprise. "Oh, Sophie. I take that back. You're a naughty, blessed girl. Trying to give me a heart attack."

I closed the call and wrapped her in a warm hug. "I've missed you."

"I missed you too." She pulled away but kept my arms firmly in her grip. "Wait. You're here! I thought you swore off flying?"

"Turns out it's a beautiful drive."

"Especially for me," Tanner said with a wink. Grammy laughed as I elbowed him in the ribs. He wrapped his arm around me and kissed my head.

Grammy sighed. "It's so good to see you two together again. I knew you would come to your senses, Tanner."

Tanner wrapped his other arm around Grammy, pulling her into a side hug. "It took my mom and my brother agreeing with you to help me see reason. I didn't deserve another chance, but Sophie was kind enough to give me one anyway. She even brought me home with her for a couple of weeks so I could see the town right. No sabotage this time."

"Except for maybe your female subscribers," I said, raising my eyebrows meaningfully. He coughed to cover a laugh. They'd followed us around town, trying to catch him alone. One even tried to draw me away from him so the others could pounce, but I'd brought him with me instead and infuriated them all. It seemed the world had plenty to learn about Tanner's current status of Very Much Taken.

"It's nice of you two to visit," Grammy said. "Doing a show on a city nearby? I like the new format and your partnership. You talking about the buildings and the history, and Sophie talking about the local wildlife and plants? It's the most thorough and entertaining review of a place I've ever seen. And so adorable the way you work together."

"Viewers seem to love it too," Tanner said. "Ratings are almost double what they were. I think the whole world has fallen for Sophie, and I can't blame them." He smiled at me again, a real smile, the one he reserved especially for me.

"Actually," I said, turning back to Grammy, "we're here for

another purpose too. We wanted you to be the first to know. Well, the second because Carmen knows too." I lifted my hand. There on my third finger rested a golden band carved to look like the branches of a tree. In the center was a leaf with a diamond inside. He'd had it custom made. I loved that nobody else in the world had an engagement ring exactly like this.

"What?" Grammy exclaimed, pulling us both into a tight hug that nearly crushed my ribs. "When did this happen? You could have gotten me involved, Tanner. I thought you would at least record the whole thing for your channel."

"So much of our lives is public," he said, still looking at me. "We wanted this part to be just between us. Although there may have been some curious animals nearby who witnessed it."

"He proposed in the Redwoods," I explained. "Right in the middle of a giant tree. It wasn't the Loch Ness Monster or anything, but I figured it would do."

Grammy clapped her hands together. "So the question is, where do you plan to live?"

"Huckleberry Creek, of course," Tanner said. "We bought a lot right on the lake, and the house plans are being approved right now."

"I love the old house, but we wanted something of our own," I told her. "Carmen is going to rent it with a couple of roommates. You don't mind, do you?"

"Of course not. It sounds beautiful. And the show?"

Tanner shrugged. "We'll travel for three months to gather material, then return to rest for three months. That way we can edit and post videos without subscribers chasing us from place to place, all cozy in the peace and quiet of home."

Home. The way he said it made my entire body warm. We could travel every single day, and I'd still feel at home with him.

"Let me guess," Grammy said. "The wedding will be in Huckleberry Creek too?"

"Carmen is already hard at work planning a wedding everyone will remember," I said, "in Four Seasons Park. We're re-creating my parents' wedding since it brought us back together."

Grammy looked a little teary. "It's perfect. Absolutely perfect. I'm so happy for you."

"There's only one thing missing," I told her. "Would you walk me down the aisle?"

She smiled, her eyes glistening. "Of course. I'd be honored."

"Actually, there's another thing I can't believe nobody has mentioned," Tanner said. "We're in Florida and we haven't had any Mexican food yet. I hear it's extra spicy here, which as Sophie knows is my very favorite. What do you say we go out for dinner? My treat."

As Grammy laughed, I took Tanner's hand, feeling his fingers rub along the diamond on my finger. Then I contentedly rested my head against his shoulder. "There's nothing I'd like more."

JOIN Sasha's newsletter and get *A Not-So-Perfect Wedding: A Four Seasons Park Short* (the story of Tanner and Sophie's wedding day) in minutes!

A Not-so-Perfect WEDDING

a Four Seasons Park short

SASHA HART

Want a free Four Seasons Park Short that you can't get anywhere else? (Hint: It's about Tanner & Sophie's wedding and things don't go...let's say, *exactly* as planned.)

Join Sasha's newsletter at SashaHart.com and get it in your inbox within minutes—and you won't miss a single release in the series!

Preorder JUST SAY SNOW TO A SECOND CHANCE now!

Corie is a Manhattan reporter with a big dream—to make an author appearance on Wake Up, America. Soon the entire country will see her as a romance expert. Even the biggest event she's ever covered—the wedding of celebrity Tanner Carmichael and Sophie Goodman—can't deter her from boycotting romance for her dream. She's found something far better.

But when her roommate drags her to a Colorado ski resort for Christmas, she runs into the last guy she ever wanted to see again—her high school ex and first love. The one she never quite got over. Worse, he's all grown up in a really, *really* good way.

So when a storm hits and forces them to rely on one another to survive the night, she's forced to face emotions that contradict everything she wrote in her relationships book. Can Corie learn from the broken relationships of her past and find the courage to try one more time?

(This is a full-length novel with some content previously published as *Love Right: A Sweet Romance Novella*)
Preorder your copy now!

ABOUT THE AUTHOR

SASHA HART loves watching, reading, and writing sweet romantic comedies with swoon-worthy happily-ever-afters and all the feels. Visit her at SashaHart.com.

Before You Go

Don't forget
to leave
a review!
(Thank you!)

♥ ♥ ♥ ♥ ♥

Made in the USA
Columbia, SC
22 December 2022